Poustinia:
A Novel

Kathleen McKee

Dedication

Poustinia: A Novel is dedicated to the Sisters of I.H.M. who taught me to be a woman of strength, conviction, and fortitude.

May their legacy of educating our future leaders sustain their mission and extend their ministry for years to come.

Prologue

Victoria peered out gingerly from behind Adirondack curtains, trying to see into the darkness. The wind whined as it bent boughs of oak and maple saplings that grew near the rustic cabin. Every rustle of leaves and creaking branch made her a little more nervous about her sojourn to the woods.

Victoria stepped back and glanced around the one room poustinia. That's what the brochure called it—a poustinia. Strange sounding name or not, why would a single woman want to stay alone in a cabin for a week, her friends questioned. Myra, her 60-something neighbor, admonished her repeatedly for the last 3 weeks, although she good naturedly agreed to take in her mutt, Harvey.

The room looked recently cleaned and smelled fresh. There was a single bed with a cozy comforter and two big fluffy pillows, with its headboard at the back wall. Next to the bed was a nightstand with enough room for the few books she brought to catch up on her reading, and a single lamp that seemed to give good light over the bed. A few feet away was a small bathroom with a shower, toilet, and pedestal sink.

By the front door, to the right, were the one window and a small writing desk and chair. To the left was a little kitchenette with a single cook top, microwave, and mini-refrigerator. The cabinets, Victoria observed, had a set of dishes and a few pots and pans, all stacked neatly, with a stool at the side of the counter. Victoria wondered if the last visitor had even used the equipment, chuckling to herself at the vision of some poor delivery kid traipsing through the woods to deliver a pizza.

Victoria peered out the window again, looking at the thickening ominous clouds. Even though the window had a screen, she was too afraid of the brewing storm and deep darkness to open it. She was glad to have a big ceiling fan with a center lamp to circulate some air and light up the cabin.

Myra was right. What possessed her to pick up that brochure and decide that she needed a retreat in the dark of nowhere? She had been feeling out of sorts lately. Always the steady and sure one, Victoria seemed uncertain about the future, and was becoming more aware of growing older. She no longer seemed to have the energy she used to, or even the desire to stay at the top of the corporate ladder.

She had seen the brochure in a colorful little pouch on the bulletin board when she was waiting in line at the post office. Three people in line ahead of her each had a bunch of parcels to mail; insurance on this one, but not that one, delivery confirmation here, but not there. All she needed was a book of stamps, but she was feeling impatient that, once again, she was waiting for people who seemed to have nothing better to do than count out their quarters and dimes at the counter.

Victoria tried to focus on the bulletin board. There was a picture of a small white cat. In screaming neon letters, the sign advertised a reward for the feline that had wandered out of the yard. She looked at the seedy characters on the FBI Most Wanted posters, all tacked neatly in a row, and wondered how often any of them ever got removed.

As the line slowly advanced, Victoria reached for one of the brochures in the packet. The front cover had a picture of a quaint little cabin nestled among tall trees, with a pebble-stone walkway leading to a covered porch. Two white rocking chairs and a flower box at the window made an attractive backdrop. Bright colored pansies seemed shaded from the warmth of the sun, and invited the weary guest to rest awhile, away from the hustle and bustle of a frenzied world.

The brochure drew her in and settled her impatience. "Discern where life is leading you," it said. "Come to the Poustinias at the Monastery of St. Carmella, nestled in 383 acres of forest and vineyards. Walk along the stream that feeds the small mountain lake. For the hardy soul, take a dip in the invigorating water that promises to whisk away the cares of the world."

Victoria snapped out of her reverie with the seemingly abrupt words of the postmaster. "What can I do for you, lady?" She quickly paid for her stamps, threw the brochure into her purse and headed toward the door.

"By the way, ma'am," he called after her. "I've heard that's a real nice place up in the country. Those nuns make the best wine around here."

The next few days were really busy ones for Victoria. She had forgotten about the brochure until she noticed it peeking from her pocketbook one evening after a particularly grueling day. On a whim, she decided to call the number even though the staff had probably long since closed shop for the day. Surprisingly, her call was answered on the second ring. "Monastery of St. Carmella; Sister Antoinette speaking."

The Sister was charming and told Victoria about the accommodations, the cost, and the availability of one of the cabins. "There are five poustinias in our wooded area, and they're quite popular. Perhaps you know that a poustinia is a place of solitude. We hope that our guests find the ambiance conducive to reflection and discernment."

As an afterthought, she added, "Safety's not an issue. The monastery property is surrounded by a wrought-iron fence, and the gate is locked at night. Each cabin has a small refrigerator, a cook-top stove, and a microwave oven, as well as some basic cooking utensils and dishes, but you'll want to bring your own groceries."

Victoria booked the next available cabin, the last week of June.

Chapter 1

Myra still didn't seem to understand my decision to rough it for a week. When I brought Harvey to her house with his kibbles, treats, and leash, she again tried to talk me out of the nonsensical idea. "Tell me again why...," she began, but stopped when she glanced at my admonishing look. Harvey didn't seem to like the idea either. Although he liked Myra, he knew the grocery bags by the front door meant that he was staying.

"You've got my house key, in case I forgot something," I said. "You can either hold my mail or throw it on my kitchen table if you want to get it out of your way."

"You do realize you're not going to have a TV out there. I can't imagine not watching my shows."

"I'll get along fine. I'm not bringing my laptop, and I'll only check my voicemail once a day."

"Well, at least let me know that you arrived safely," Myra called out to me as I got into the car. I heard Harvey give one of those sad hound dog howls as I pulled away. It broke my heart, but the Sister said no pets were allowed.

The drive to the monastery was a nice one, once I got out of traffic. It was a perfect summer day, with a cobalt blue sky and wispy clouds, probably a little shy of 80 degrees. I could feel the tension in my shoulders wane a little as I turned off the expressway and let the GPS guide me to the back roads leading to the countryside. I carefully followed the drone of "In 800 yards, turn right, then turn left."

I decided to forego the music station on the radio so I wouldn't miss a turn. When I heard, "You have reached your destination," I felt certain there was some error until I noticed an imposing gate with very simple wrought iron lettering that read *Monastery of St. Carmella*. It was almost hidden in the shadows of the trees.

I drove carefully through the gate, somewhat in awe of the winding drive. Beautiful perennials lined both sides, and I noticed how well kept they were. I thought of all the weeds that had popped up in my front garden after it had looked so fresh in late spring. Obviously someone at the monastery enjoyed gardening.

At the last curve, I saw a beautiful stone *porte couchère* and front entrance to a breathtaking mansion. It was easy to imagine a gentleman farmer bequeathing his country estate to the nuns a century ago. Of course, that's how my imagination works. Maybe when the old Sisters were young, they hauled rocks from the creek bed and hired local stonemasons and carpenters to build a majestic home large enough for a winery and a monastery. This is a pretty cool place, I thought, as I rang the bell at the front door.

It didn't take long for an older woman to respond. "I'm Victoria Sullivan. I have a reservation for a cabin."

"And I'm Sister Antoinette. We spoke on the phone. I'm so happy to meet you, Victoria."

I was rather surprised that she didn't look anything like I expected. She had attractively styled white hair and wore a pretty pant suit that looked decidedly upscale department store quality.

"Let's do the paperwork and get you settled into your poustinia for the week."

I followed Sister Antoinette to her office, the first room on the right, across from a beautiful, grand staircase. The office was massive, with a wood burning fireplace at one end, large double paned arched windows along the entire outer wall, and built-in bookcases. There was a cozy sitting area by the fireplace consisting of a sofa, coffee table, and two large recliners. A large oak desk faced the entrance, with two upholstered Queen Anne chairs in front of the desk. Sister Antoinette invited me to have a seat as she explained the rental agreement.

As I was signing the documents, Sister Antoinette processed my credit card. It felt as if I were finalizing arrangements at a five-star hotel, rather than a rustic cabin in the woods.

"How did you hear about our poustinias, Victoria?"

I told Sister Antoinette about seeing the brochures in my local post office, and that they had piqued my interest.

"I'm not sure what intrigued me more, the rocking chairs on the cabin porch or a week of peace and quiet. I just seem to be at a new stage of my life, and I'm not sure what direction to take."

"I know what you mean. When I was younger, I felt like I had unlimited energy. Now, by the end of the day, I'm content to spend time in our monastery chapel or relax with a good book."

"I don't know too much about nuns, but I guess I figured you don't have a lot of decisions to make."

"Well, I'm happy to tell you that I'm probably not too different from you. Regardless, I feel certain that you'll enjoy your visit with us."

It wasn't long before we were ready. Sister Antoinette noted that there was a small parking lot across from the monastery where I could park my car and gather my bags. She helped me put them into a golf cart, and spryly jumped into the driver's side. No wonder the nun was tired by the end of the day.

"Hop in. I'll take you to the cabin. It's not far, but too much when you have a suitcase and food for the week."

Sister Antoinette expertly maneuvered the golf cart and gave a brief tour of the property. She explained that the five camp sites were fairly close, but each was situated far enough away that it couldn't be seen from the others. Each had a land line phone that connected directly to the monastery in case of an emergency, or the need for a ride to the parking lot.

"Some folks want complete privacy, while others are not used to the quiet, and want to head into town for some excitement."

I couldn't quite imagine what kind of excitement could be in any of the little towns I had passed through on the way.

"Oh, and there's an outlet mall only about 30 miles west." She winked. I'm sure it was a wink. I could picture a van load of nuns on a Saturday excursion.

"Well, here we are."

My cabin looked just like the picture on the brochure, and I loved the little front porch. I knew I was going to spend a lot of time in the rocking chair.

After unloading the cart and showing me where the battery lanterns were kept in case the power went out, Sister Antoinette gave me a warm smile and said, "You call me if you need anything. If I'm not there, ask one of the nuns to get Tony. That's me. I'll be here in a flash." I decided I liked this lady.

Chapter 2

W hen I saw the ominous clouds and darkening skies, I was kicking myself for not listening to the radio on my way to the monastery. Obviously there was a storm brewing. I took the two lanterns out from under the kitchenette sink, just to be sure they worked.

I called Myra to tell her that I had arrived safely and to see how Harvey was doing. She said he had settled in pretty quickly and was snoozing by her seat on the sofa. I didn't tell her about the nervousness I was now feeling because I didn't want another lecture. Instead, I highlighted the beautiful scenery and my delightful encounter with Sister Tony.

"She sounds nice. Maybe this will be a good get-away for you after all."

Myra sounded pretty laid back tonight. I guess Harvey was working his magic. We chatted a little longer before I disconnected, remembering to put my phone on the charger.

I could hear the rain begin its cadence when a sudden clap of thunder startled me. Beyond the howling of the wind seemed to come a loud wail and then a bang at the door. I wondered if a large branch had tumbled to the porch as I pulled back the curtain to peer out the window. A bright flash of lightening illuminated a bedraggled young woman, her latest yelp muffled by another loud bark of thunder.

I opened the door as quickly as I could manage, and the girl stumbled in. Together we pushed the door closed against the winds, and flinched at another flash of lightening. I turned and looked at her as she stood trembling. It seemed like she was trying to hold the storm at bay, panting long, deep breaths with intermittent sighs.

I pulled out the desk chair and invited her to sit while I made a cup of tea for each of us. As the kettle was heating, I got a towel from the bathroom, and noted that her breathing was becoming less labored. She looked up at me with big brown eyes, streaked with heavy mascara.

"I'm Amanda Angeli, and I'm staying in the next cabin. I'm really scared of storms."

"I'm happy to meet you, Amanda Angeli. I'm Victoria Sullivan, and I'm not too crazy about them myself."

While Amanda dried herself with the towel, I found two mugs in the kitchen cabinet and steeped the tea. Amanda couldn't be more than a teenager, maybe 17 or 18 years old, with a slender and petite build. She had long, straight brown hair with a streak of neon pink and green; a jeweled nose piercing was in her left nostril. As she dried her hair, I also observed five matching jewel posts in each ear, and wondered what else might be pierced.

"So, Amanda Angeli, what brings you here to the monastery poustinias?"

She shrugged. "You can call me Amanda, just Amanda."

"OK, just Amanda, are you staying in the next cabin by yourself?"

She didn't seem to think that my attempt at humor was amusing, but she nodded yes. Amanda looked at me with penetrating eyes, seeming to identify me as someone she could trust, at least a little.

"My father brought me here a few days ago." I noticed the tongue piercing. "He said I needed some time alone and to grow up, whatever that means. I think he just wanted to get me away from my friends and out of the house so he could get it on with his secretary."

I nodded, watching her body language. She seemed to be doing the same thing to me.

I decided not to push her for details, and moved the conversation to a lighter note. I told her about finding the poustinia brochure on the post office bulletin board and how my neighbor, Myra, thought I was crazy to spend a week of precious vacation time in a monastery cabin.

"The only thing I'm missing is my dog, Harvey," I said. "He's good company, and he'd have loved a week chasing squirrels in the woods."

In the next hour, as the storm was waning, Amanda and I chatted about Harvey's antics and her memories of wanting a puppy when she was a youngster. She told me that she was an only child, and had a close relationship with her mother. Her father was a history professor who was always engrossed in his books, doing research, or marking papers. I got the feeling that he was somewhat distant.

Before long, we both realized that the storm had passed, and we had enjoyed each other's company. I opened the door to feel the gentle breeze, and noted the fresh smell of rain-soaked leaves and flowers.

"Would you like me to walk you back to your cabin, Amanda?" She assured me that she was fine now, although she accepted my offer of one of the lanterns to help guide her along the path.

Chapter 3

I awoke to a cacophony of chirping and glanced at my watch. Still on work time. I stretched under the warm comforter, hearing caws and twitters, and even the hoot of an owl in the distance. My brain seemed to resist my body's urging for another hour of sleep. I threw off the covers and heated the kettle while I showered and dressed. The cabin was a little chilly, so I put on jeans and a sweatshirt and double checked the inside of my sneakers to make sure that no creepy crawlers had invaded them during the night.

After opening the curtains and straightening the bed, I took my tea to the front porch and sat in the comfy rocking chair. Rejecting the impulse to see if I had any voice messages, I closed my eyes and breathed in the crisp, fresh air. If I listened carefully, I could hear little critters scurrying through the underbrush. It was a delightfully peaceful feeling.

By the time my tea was finished, I was ready for my first exploration of the countryside. I walked down the path, trying to retrace some of the sights that Sister Tony had pointed out the day before. I decided to stay on the well-traveled road until I reached the vineyard. Rows and rows of carefully tended vines seemed to be bursting with clusters of unripened grapes. The nuns will be making lots of wine this year, I chuckled to myself. I pictured huge vats of grapes, with barefooted nuns, long dresses and aprons hiked up and tied around the waist, stomping out the juice like the "I Love Lucy" classic.

"It really is a beautiful sight, isn't it?" I turned to see a woman about my age standing behind me.

"I didn't mean to startle you," she said.

"Are you one of the Sisters?"

She laughed, a hearty chuckle. "No, but I almost could be one." I noticed deep smile lines around her pretty eyes. "I come here to the poustinias every chance I get. I'm Elizabeth Sweeney. Please call me Betty."

"Hi, Betty. I'm Victoria Sullivan. This is my first time."

"Ah, the first time will make or break you."

I wasn't too sure what she meant by that. She must have read my mind.

"Oh, I meant that in a good way. Some people love the quiet, and others hate it."

"You sound like Sister Tony."

"Well, if you get bored, there's an outlet mall about 30 miles west of here." We both laughed.

"Would you like me to show you the best part of this place?" Betty asked.

"I'd love it!"

We both kept pace along the road, then Betty led me to a small path in the woods, just beyond the vineyard. She showed me the creek that was nestled among the trees. We stopped to rest on the trunk of a big fallen tree that seemed perfectly fitted along the bank. I noticed that the water gurgled past large boulders, but it wasn't too deep. I could see a murky bottom and a few bubbles every now and then.

"This is a beautiful spot," I sighed contentedly.

"This is," Betty agreed, "but the best is yet to come. I usually stop here to catch my breath, and take some time to clear my head. I'm a lawyer, and my life is pretty hectic. My brain seems to never stop until I come here and begin to unload and debrief."

We sat in silence, and I could feel my own thoughts begin to wane. Again, I closed my eyes and listened to the sounds around me.

Betty and I both seemed ready to move on about the same time, and we continued our journey along the creek. It seemed odd to me that the brush was cleared out along the bank, but I realized that this path must be fairly well-traveled. Before long, the forest opened to a beautiful lake.

"Ta-da!" Betty exclaimed.

"Wow!" was all I could say.

It wasn't a huge lake, as I could see the sloping banks on the distant side. There was an anchored wooden raft in the center of the lake. It looked like someone was fishing off the side.

"That's Charlie," Betty said. "He stays in the farthest cabin in the woods and keeps pretty much to himself. He's a strange old coot; doesn't talk much. Sometimes I wonder if he lives here, because he's here every time I come. I don't know if he catches anything, but I'll often see him fishing out there. I'm guessing he leaves his fishing gear on the raft and swims out there each morning. I don't know how he does it because, let me tell you, that water is downright frigid!"

We found a nice clearing and sat on the beach. The sun was warm, but the humidity was low, and there was still a gentle breeze.

"Sister Tony told me that the early sisters dammed the creek," Betty explained. "She said in those days they had a bunch of novices, and the young sisters could swim for their recreation each afternoon. Apparently, they'd work in the vineyards all morning, come in for their noon prayers and lunch, and then race each other to the lake."

I could picture the scene like one of those old fashioned sepia postcards showing a bunch of young women posing on the beach, proudly displaying their bloomers and bathing caps.

"Tell me more about Charlie out there," I said.

"Not much to tell. I asked Sister Tony about him, but she didn't give me any details. She just said that he had a tough life, and liked to come here to fish and take care of the flowers. End of story."

"Maybe he killed someone, and is doing penance for the rest of his life."

"You do have a vivid imagination!" Betty said. I heartily agreed.

The sun was high in the sky by the time we brushed off our pants and headed back to the cabins. Betty took me on a different path that led through the woods. The shade was refreshing after the warmth on the beach. Betty pointed through the trees.

"If you look past that notch, you'll see the cabin that Charlie stays in."

"Wow, that's pretty secluded."

Betty chuckled and said, "Sister Tony puts the newbies in the cabins closest to the road. I think there's some kid in the cabin near you, and I saw a young woman on the porch of the cabin between us. I haven't met them yet."

"I met the kid last night. She was afraid of the storm. Actually, I wasn't too keen on it either."

"That was a whopper. I think being in the woods just intensifies the sounds. So, who's the kid?"

"Her name's Amanda. She said that her dad brought her here to get her away from her friends. You know, she looks like a tough street punk, with her neon hair and piercings, but she really is sweet."

"I see kids like that in juvenile court. They get with the wrong crowd and, before you know it, they're headed down a long and rocky road. Sometimes intervention works, sometimes it doesn't. It's really sad."

"I like Amanda. She's spunky, if not in a rebellious way. But I'm not sure that I agree with the idea of shipping her off to a cabin in the woods so she can grow up."

"I'm surprised Sister Tony agreed to that. There must be something Amanda didn't tell you."

"Oh, I'm sure there's plenty. I didn't press her for details."

"Here's where we part," Betty said as we neared a fork in the path. My cabin's about 200 feet that way. You turn to the left and then just stay on the path. You'll be back to your place in no time at all."

"I'm really happy we met."

"Me, too," Betty replied. "Catch you later!"

∧∧∧

I was tired when I got back to my cabin. Although I try to stay in shape, it's been quite a while since I had such a workout. Once I had the back yard fenced, Harvey and I didn't take many walks. He wasn't the easiest mutt to walk, and I was usually weary after a long day's work.

I rooted through the bags of food I had brought and found one of those microwavable meals that doesn't need refrigeration or freezing. By the time the microwave dinged, I had poured a glass of soda from one of the two-liter bottles I had stacked in the mini fridge last night. I pulled the stool up to the counter and tried not to eat too quickly. I set up two empty bags, one for trash and one for recycling, and cleaned up before pouring another cold one.

The afternoon sun made the porch a little too warm, but I opened the window to get some fresh air before washing up and changing into a lighter t-shirt. I sat at the desk with one of the books I had brought and had barely read the first chapter when I heard footsteps on the wooden porch.

"Hey, Vicki. You in there?"

I opened the front door to see Amanda with the lantern in her hand. I welcomed her, and held my tongue about the Vicki thing.

"Where've you been? I came by earlier but you weren't here."

I told her about my exploration to the lake, and meeting up with Betty.

"I've been there. Did you see that creepy guy fishing?"

"I saw someone fishing. What makes you think he's creepy?"

"I tried to get him to talk to me the other day when he was weeding the flowers by the monastery. He was rude, and wouldn't even look at me. He's a jerk."

"Well, maybe he's hard of hearing, or had something on his mind."

"Nah, he's a creep. I don't understand why the nuns let him stay here."

I decided to change the subject.

"So, Amanda, what did you do today?"

"I slept until 11:30, then came to see you. Since you weren't here, I went back to my cabin and made a peanut butter and jelly sandwich. Then I wrote in my journal for a while. I brought back your lantern."

"So I noticed. Thank you. Do you want something cold to drink? I have some soda and powdered iced tea mix."

Amanda decided on the iced tea. She pulled the stool over to the desk.

"Tell me about this Betty lady. Is she the old one or the younger one?"

"I guess she's the old one, because she's about my age—but I don't think of myself as old."

Amanda gave me a sheepish grin and said, "I didn't mean it like that. I don't think of you as old either, although you remind me of a grandmother like I always wanted."

"You don't have a grandmother?"

"Not that I know of. My dad's parents died when he was a kid, and my mother never spoke about her parents. I asked her once, but she just said it was a long story, and someday she'd tell me about it. Then she died."

"Your mom passed away?"

"Yeah, she died two years ago. It's no big deal. We didn't even have a funeral. Dad and I just went to the grave and watched them bury her coffin. Then we went home."

I didn't know what to say.

As if coming out of her reverie, Amanda suddenly said, "Hey, Vic."

"Victoria," I replied.

"Whatever. You got a cell phone?"

"Yes."

"Can I use it?"

"Why?" Amanda seemed to switch on an attitude, and I wasn't so sure I liked this new persona.

"I need to let my friends know where I am."

"Why don't you use the phone in your cabin?"

I knew full well that Amanda's father wanted her away from the influence of her friends. I certainly didn't want to be a co-conspirator.

"Are you kidding? It's hooked up to the nuns' switchboard at the monastery. Whoever answers would probably tell that kookie Tony. She's weird."

"Why do you think she's weird?"

"I think she spies on me, then she probably calls my dad to tell him what I've been doing. Sometimes she brings me stuff like dinner or a sandwich. She makes it look like she's just being nice, but I see her eyes wandering, looking around to see what I'm doing. This place is driving me nuts. Let me just call Derek."

"Who's Derek?"

"He's the guy I go with. He's probably getting pretty mad that I haven't responded to any of his messages."

"How do you know he's left you any messages?" Amanda gave me one of those looks of disdain.

"No," I said firmly. "You may not use my phone."

"Did you bring a computer?"

"No, I decided not to do any..." I didn't have a chance to finish my sentence. Amanda stormed out, slamming the door behind her.

Chapter 4

It's her loss, I thought to myself as I stared at the door. Why was I left with such a sense of unease? I tried to settle my discomfort by reminding myself that I was here to relax and unwind, not get embroiled in someone else's drama.

I picked up my book and went out to the porch. The waning afternoon sun was slipping beyond the trees, and I settled into my favorite spot. I couldn't quite get focused on my reading, so I closed my eyes and rocked. I could feel myself drifting into a little nap.

Twenty minutes later and much more refreshed, I awoke to the sounds of the golf cart pulling up. "Hi, Victoria!" called a familiar voice.

"It's nice to see you, Sister Tony."

"I don't usually disturb our guests, but I brought something for you."

I watched to see if the Sister was snooping, but there was no sign of furtive eyes. She was looking directly at me.

"We had a recent donation to benefit the poustinias, so each cabin is getting a small end table for the porch." I helped her unload the table and set it by my rocking chair.

"Some of our visitors have noted that the cabins can get stuffy with only one window, so we're installing screen doors on each poustinia. You can choose to have it installed while you're here, or we can wait until you leave."

I didn't even have to think about it. "I'd love a screen door. That's a great addition!"

"Wonderful. We'll have it installed tomorrow. So, are you enjoying your stay?"

I told Sister Tony about meeting up with Betty at the vineyards and our jaunt to the lake. For some reason I didn't tell her about Amanda.

"You'll like Betty. She comes here as often as she can get away from her hectic schedule. I have a feeling that the two of you have a lot in common. Now I've got to get going. We have Vespers at 5:00 p.m., followed by dinner. Give me a call if you need anything. And don't worry if you're out walking when our handyman hangs the door. He's fast and reliable, and he won't want to disturb you."

I sat there a little while longer, mulling about my first 24 hours in the woods. Amanda's a piece of work. In some ways, she's a tough punk, testing her limits and pushing others away. But underneath that façade is a young woman who needs direction and love. Betty's friendly and outgoing, yet comes to the monastery every chance she gets. I definitely wanted to know more about her. Charlie seems to be an interesting character, and I wondered why he hung around the monastery. And Sister Tony... She must be in charge of the poustinias, but she doesn't exactly seem nunly—whatever that means. Maybe I would meet some of the other Sisters through the week.

As dusk arrived, I brought my book inside and foraged for another microwavable meal. Turning on the desk lamp, I closed the window, pulled the curtain, and ate at the counter. I had to admit, the poustinia was rather cozy, and I didn't even miss the usual evening drone of a TV. I read a few chapters of my book, then hit the sack.

^^^

I slept soundly through the night, which rather surprised me because I often sleep fitfully, waking up, focusing on a problem at work, then can't get back to sleep. It felt good to awake refreshed and ready to start the day.

I took a quick shower, fixed the bed, and zapped a bagel after I made my tea. Breakfast for a king—or queen, I chuckled to myself, searching for a little jelly packet. I had to give myself credit for my meal-planning skills.

I checked my voicemail. Myra called to say that Harvey was behaving, and my administrative assistant let me know that she was handling my e-mails and calls at work. I flipped off the phone and put it in my pocket, ready to plan my day.

My schedule included reading in the morning, lunch around noon, changing to a bathing suit, and walking to the lake after lunch. I'd stay there for a few hours of sunbathing, then back to the cabin for a shower and change of clothes. After supper, I'd walk to the monastery and take a look around. That sounded pretty good to me.

I grabbed my book and tea, and went out to the porch. Ten minutes later, I saw Betty coming down the path and waved her over. "Would you like a cup of tea?" She declined, explaining that she was out for her morning walk and didn't want to have to pee behind some tree. I told her about my plan to go to the lake for a swim and sunbathe after lunch, and invited her to join me.

"I could do that, but I refuse to put one toe into that freezing water." We both laughed. "So, has your little friend been back?" I knew she was referring to Amanda, so I told her about yesterday's visit.

"You were right about not giving her your phone, Victoria. She's here for a reason and it must be pretty serious. It might even be court-ordered." I hadn't thought of that.

"What I found most surprising is that Sister Tony brings Amanda lunch or dinner each day." Betty raised her eyebrows. "Well, that's what she told me."

"That's interesting," Betty said. "In all the years I've been coming here, none of the Sisters, including Sister Tony, ever intruded on my privacy. In fact, I was surprised when Sister Tony came by yesterday with the porch table, although I was so pleased with the new addition that I didn't even think about it."

"Me, too. Amanda thinks she's spying on her."

"If anything, she might be making sure she's OK. Amanda seems mighty young to be roughing it on her own."

"I know. I went off to college when I was 18, but I had a good support system, and schoolwork kept me busy. Amanda was yanked away from her friends with no means of communication. Kids today can't exist without their eyes glued to their phones, waiting for the next text to pop up."

"Kids aren't the only ones. Did you see the video of the lady who fell into an open man-hole when she was texting? She was lucky she didn't get killed!"

"I just wonder why Amanda's dad brought her here. Why not enroll her in some summer camp or pre-college program?"

"I guess because she'd have access to phones and computers there. Her dad must really want to get her away from bad influences."

"Yeah, but I'd worry more about what could happen to a young girl alone in the woods, or even if she'd hurt herself."

"She seems to trust you, Victoria. You could reach out to her."

"I'm not so sure about that. She stormed out of my cabin with quite an attitude when I told her that she couldn't use my phone."

Betty seemed to be analyzing the situation. "I think she'll come around. You protected her when she was frightened. That's a more powerful memory than the 'no' to her request for the phone."

While I chewed on that tidbit, Betty said she was off for her morning constitution. "I'll meet you at the lake around 1 p.m. Don't forget your sunblock!"

Chapter 5

I got to the beach first, and noticed that the anchored lake platform was empty. Testing the water, I wondered if I could still swim that far. With the evening temperatures dropping down to the 50's, and the lake being spring-fed, I figured it would probably be late August before the lake would be warm enough to swim. I spread out my towel on the beach, and got comfortably arranged. Rolling the clothes I'd worn over my bathing suit made a good pillow. It wasn't long before Betty arrived.

"Couldn't do it, huh?" Betty asked as she spread her towel. "Your suit's not even wet."

"I will, one of these days. Where's Charlie?"

"I saw him drive away this morning when I was walking past the monastery. Maybe he went to town to get some supplies, or maybe he wrapped up his stay."

"Amanda said she thinks he's creepy. She said she tried to engage him in conversation, but he totally ignored her."

"Mmmmm," Betty agreed lazily. "He's a man of few words."

We both got lost in our worlds for a few moments. I think I even dozed. When I opened my eyes, Betty was gazing across the lake.

"Have you ever been married, Victoria?"

"No, never met the right guy. How about you?"

"I was married to my college sweetheart for 34 years. John died of an aneurysm 4 years ago. Just suddenly keeled over and he was gone. The doctors said there was nothing anyone could have done to bring him back. If he'd gone for an annual checkup like I always reminded him to do, maybe they would have found it. They could have done surgery to repair it." She shook her head like she was still in disbelief.

"I'm so sorry, Betty." I reached over to touch her hand. "Not only was his death a shock, but you lost your best friend. Tell me about him."

"John was my strength. My friends say it was the other way around, but they're wrong. We met in law school and got married shortly after graduation. We didn't have much money in those days, what with student loans and studying for the bar exam, but we both passed after the first try and got hired at different firms. I went to work with the county as a public defender; John grabbed a spot with a prestigious group in the city. The first couple of years were tough, and we floundered a little at times, but we always got back on track."

"Did you have any children?"

"No, that was one of the rough spots. I really wanted a baby, so I kept nagging him that we needed to slow down to start a family. He wasn't as committed, even though we had previously agreed on two children. When I couldn't get pregnant, he said we could adopt, but I wasn't ready to raise another woman's baby. Now that I'm older and wiser, I would have agreed. There are so many unwanted babies who need a mother."

"So, you both got busy with work?"

"We did. But we were lucky. We bought a reasonably priced home that suited our needs, and we paid off our student loans. We began to do *pro bono* work together, working with poor families who were battling prejudice and rotten luck. We discovered a lake campsite in the country, and often would take troubled kids with us on a weekend getaway. It became our mission, and the glue that kept us together all those years."

"Is that why you come here?"

"I suppose it is, in a way. We'd rent a boat for the day and fish for our supper. The lake was about this size, but instead of an anchored raft in the middle, it had a little island. We'd race to see who could be the first to the island and, after we rested along the beach, we'd leisurely paddle back. John and I used to laugh that if we got the kids tired enough, they'd be asleep by the time the camp fire died out. He was right," Betty chuckled. "Or, at least we missed any shenanigans because we fell asleep, too. And, you know what? Every one of those kids turned out all right. John really had a gift."

"Don't sell yourself short. John couldn't have done it alone." Betty looked like she was going to disagree. "You said it yourself, Betty. You both relied on each other for strength. It's what we aim for in business. Finding talent and building on it creates teamwork. You brought meaning to the lives of those kids, and had success in helping them turn their lives around. You did it together."

I looked at Betty and saw that her eyes were misty.

"I miss him so much. I come here because I can feel John here with me. Somehow, it even seems like he's speaking to me."

We sat watching the ripples on the lake, lost in our own reveries.

Eventually, Betty said, "You mentioned something about business and teamwork. Do you work in the corporate world?"

"I do. I'm Vice President of Human Resources at a publishing firm in the city."

"That sounds pretty impressive. What brought you to that line of work?"

"I've always loved books, and majored in journalism at college. After I graduated, I got a job at the firm as an editorial assistant, and worked my way up to a management position. That's when I found my true niche. I loved interviewing candidates for positions, and discovered that I had a good knack for finding the right person for the right job. I went back to school and got a master's degree in Human Resources and, eventually, I was asked to become the VP."

"Wow, the powers that be must have really seen great potential in you. Have you worked for the same publishing firm your entire career?"

"Yep, 39 years come September. I still love what I do, but it seems different now. Of course, the company has grown through the years, and that led to more positions to fill. But we live in a new age, and publishing firms are struggling to maintain a strong market, despite the trend of electronic books."

"I know what you mean," Betty said. "Most of the kids I see are using their mobile devices for reading and playing games. Heck, they even tell me that some of the textbooks from school are e-books now."

"Exactly," I replied. "I don't have a problem with it, but I like a good old fashioned book that I can keep for years to come."

"So," Betty continued, like a dog with a bone, "in all those years, you never met the right guy?"

"I met lots of guys, just not the right one. Besides, I was pretty busy, and I got tired of the dating scene. I also got a dog. It just didn't seem fair to him that I'd go out at night after he'd been alone in the house all day. Harvey likes me to stay home."

"That sounds like one spoiled dog, or at least a good excuse."

"Maybe, but I decided to stop looking. If the right guy is to come my way, then it's meant to be. If not, I'm OK with it. I have friends, and I'm happy with my social life."

"I know what you're saying. I'm not looking for anyone else myself. John and I had something very special, and I have memories to last a lifetime. Now, let's get out of this sun, and relax with a good book. The rocking chair on my porch is calling me."

^^^

When I got back to the cabin, I was happy to see that the screen door had been installed. Not only did it brighten up the room, but it also let in the fresh breezes.

Sticking to my schedule, after supper I walked down the path leading to the monastery. As I approached, I admired the beautiful stone façade on the three-story structure. There was a turret on one side, and stained glass windows adorned the left wing on the second floor. The right wing appeared to be a chapel with very ornate stained glass. I waved to two older women sitting on the side porch, and they waved back.

I meandered beyond the front portico, and started down the tree-lined winding drive I entered two days ago. Two women about my age looked like they were returning from their own evening stroll. I greeted them as they approached.

"Hi. I'm Victoria, staying in one of the cabins."

"Hi, Victoria," the taller of the two said. "I'm Sister Julie, and this is Sister Dolores. Are you enjoying your visit with us?"

"You have a beautiful place here. It's a well-kept secret."

They smiled and nodded in agreement. Sister Julie had short salt and pepper hair, but I couldn't detect a strand of gray in Sister Dolores' brown bob. Both wore slacks and a short-sleeved top.

"It looks like you found the lake," Sister Dolores noted. They didn't have to be too observant to see the sunburn I was beginning to feel.

"Do you ever go there?"

"Occasionally," Sister Julie replied. "Once we built the poustinias and began having guests, we decided that our presence would intrude on their solitude. Most of us now have jobs in some of the local towns. Dolores and I teach English to migrant workers at a nearby farm. It doesn't pay a lot, but it brings in some money to help with the bills. And it keeps us connected when we need help harvesting our grapes."

"How many Sisters live here?"

"There are 14 Sisters who live in the monastery, but we're only one branch of a global community. We've set up the second floor on the east wing as an infirmary for our older Sisters, and several Sisters were trained in nursing to care for them. Those of our aged who can, engage in prayer ministry."

Sister Julie added wistfully, "It's not quite the same as when we entered the community. In its heyday, our walls were bursting at the seams. The third floor was originally designed as a dormitory for the novices and postulants but, as our numbers dwindled, we created individual rooms for each of the Sisters."

We moved to the side of the road as we heard a car approaching from the winding drive.

"Looks like Charlie's back," Julie said.

"'Evening, Sisters... ma'am," Charlie said as he slowed to a stop. He's not as old as I had imagined, though he has a thick crop of white hair.

"On Tuesday's, Charlie goes to all the local farm stands, and gathers over-ripe produce to distribute to homeless shelters and food pantries all over the county," Dolores explained.

"I kept some tomatoes, beans, and corn for the nuns," he said. "I'll drop them off at the kitchen door."

"You're a sweetheart, Charlie," Julie smiled warmly. "We'll put them in the walk-in when we get back to the house. We enjoyed a nice catfish supper tonight, thanks to you." Dolores turned to me. "Not only does he catch them, but he scales and filets them for us."

Charlie seemed to blush. "I'd best be going, ladies. Enjoy the evening," he said as he continued up the winding drive.

He's not a big talker, I thought to myself, but he's definitely not rude.

"Does Charlie live here year round?"

Both nuns nodded, and Julie explained, "About ten years ago, Charlie appeared at our door, and volunteered to do odd jobs and gardening for us."

"Rumor has it," Dolores interrupted in a whisper, "that he knew Sister Tony before she entered the convent, but she won't confirm it."

"Anyway," Julie continued, "Charlie eventually became a fixture around here. He and Tony brainstormed the poustinia idea as a revenue source, and he designed the cabins. He actually built the first one—the one he stays in—although we contracted locally for the electricity and plumbing. Tony invited him to test out the cabin, to see if it was sustainable for year round guests, and the rest, as they say, is history."

"I think it was a brilliant idea. You had the land and its pristine amenities, and you've even done a little advertising. The brochure that I found at my local post office lured me here."

"That was Tony's idea," Dolores said. "She's a pretty astute businesswoman. She convinced a local photographer to donate his services as a tax write-off, and then Charlie took the advertisements around to all of the post offices within a two-hour radius. We now have guests practically year round."

I nodded thoughtfully. "There's definitely a market. People want to get away from the rat race, unwind, and enjoy nature at its best."

"It's not for everyone, but it's been good for us."

We said our good-byes, and I continued my walk to the main road. As dusk descended, and the mosquitoes came out in full force, I decided to head back to the cabin.

Chapter 6

After my tea and bagel the next morning, I worked on my schedule for the day. I decided that I'd take a drive into town. I wanted to explore a bit of the local scene, and find a place where I could get a hat and some lotion for my sunburn. In the meantime, I gave Myra a quick call to check on Harvey. She assured me that he was adjusting well, and she had even started taking him on walks. We chatted a bit, and I told her of my plan for the day.

"Aha! You're getting stir crazy already."

"Not yet. I must admit, I miss that mutt a bit, but I'm really enjoying the peace and serenity here. Give my boy a big 'ole smooch!" I grabbed my purse, put my phone in the side pocket, and meandered to the car.

I was about two miles down the road when I spotted a young woman walking along the shoulder. A tuft of neon hair blew across her face as I drove by. I pulled over to stop ahead of her and called out the window, "Hey, Amanda. Jump in!"

She looked like she wanted to bolt, a kind of "deer-in-the-headlights" expression. She must have thought better of it, and tentatively opened the passenger side door.

"Where are you headed?"

"Nowhere."

I ignored Amanda's seeming lack of conversation and said, "I'm going into town. Would you like to join me? Maybe we can find a place to get some lunch. My treat. I actually have no idea where I'm going, but this road has to lead to somewhere."

The speed limit decreased to 35 mph, so I figured we were coming into town. It wasn't much, but I saw a gas station, a small pharmacy, a beauty salon, and a hardware store. I pulled into a parking spot in front of the pharmacy.

"I need to get a few things. Would you like to join me?"

"Whatever."

A little bell alerted the woman at the counter as we walked through the front door. She was chatting with one of the few customers and looked up.

"May I help you?" she asked.

We followed her directions to the skin creams, and passed a small display of visors and baseball caps. I tried on one of the visors, and Amanda burst out laughing.

"What's so funny?" I asked, glad that the ice was breaking.

"You're not serious!"

"I like it," I replied, adjusting the visor and looking in the little mirror on the display.

"That's really lame," Amanda said, trying on a baseball cap. She pulled out a few neon strands of hair, and checked her reflection.

"It becomes you. Let's get these."

Amanda tried to convince me that the ball cap would be more attractive, but I declined. I'd been thinking along the lines of a wide-brimmed straw hat, but the visor would serve its purpose. We selected a few more items, including a bag of chips and some candy bars for Amanda, and took our wares to the counter.

"Is there any place that we could get some lunch?" I asked the clerk.

"Jake's Diner is about a mile down Main Street, on your right. He's got a pretty good menu."

The diner was easy to find, and the parking lot was almost full. Just about every seat at the counter was taken, but we found a small booth toward the back. A waitress appeared in no time. She handed us each a menu, and gave us each a glass of ice water with lemon.

"You folks new in town?"

"We're just passing through."

"Well, we're glad you stopped by. I'm Sue, and I'll be back to take your order. We've got chili as our special today."

After spending some time reviewing the menu, I decided on a Caesar chicken salad, and Amanda chose a hamburger and fries.

"I'm sorry," Amanda said simply as she took her first bite of burger.

"Apology accepted. And what did you do yesterday?"

"Not much. I wrote in my journal and read a book. It actually was pretty good. Sister Tony must have left it on the porch. It was kind of like a murder mystery where this lady finds a skull on the beach, and some hot shot detective tries to solve the crime. They fall in love. I figured they would. Did you ever fall in love, Vicki?"

"Victoria." I replied. "And, yes, several times."

Amanda looked at me with surprise. "Really?" she asked, as if that were so far-fetched. "Did you ever get married?"

"No, that wasn't in the cards."

"Why not?"

I wasn't sure I liked this turn of conversation.

"I really don't know. My first love was in college, but we had different interests, and eventually grew apart. His name was Phillip, and he married some rich girl whose father was his first boss. I heard he's on his third wife now." I added in a hushed voice, "Am I lucky, or what?" We both laughed.

"So, who was your second love, and why didn't that work out?"

I gazed at a picture on the wall across the room, as I reflected back in time. "My second love was Kenny. We were both in our early 30's, and met at a business conference, though we both worked in the same city. We liked the same things—books, theater, visiting museums. We had talked about marriage, but he got an offer to head a new company out west. I encouraged him to take the job. It was a great opportunity for him, and I figured we could maintain a long distance relationship while he got established."

I paused, thinking of the day he left.

"And…," Amanda prompted.

"And, it didn't work out. We both were extremely busy building our careers, and our visits and phone calls became less frequent as time went on. He stayed on the west coast, and married a gal he met out there; I stayed on the east coast, and worked my way up in the corporate world. I saw him at a conference in Chicago a few years back and met his wife. They're perfect for each other, and have two great kids who are now in college. Things work out the way they're meant to."

"I'm not going to let that happen to me. I'm going to get married and have babies, and live in a nice house with a pool in the backyard. My husband's going to make a lot of money, and I'm going to stay home and make sure our family stays together."

We both mulled over her words.

"Derek's going to make a lot of money. He already does. He showed me a stack of money once, and I even saw some $100's at the bottom of the pile."

"What's he do?"

"I don't know exactly, but he's pretty good with fixing up old cars. He said he'd take care of the money stuff, and I can make the babies. Didn't you ever want to have a baby?"

"Sure. That's how most of us are wired. I wanted a boy and a girl, in that order. How about you?"

"I'm thinking at least 6 kids. I don't care if they're boys or girls, but lots of girls could help around the house. The boys could help Derek."

"It sounds like you'll be a pretty busy mom. Do you want any dessert?"

"Yeah, I'd like a hot fudge sundae. How about you?"

"I'm watching my girlish figure, but I'll have a spoonful of yours."

"That's a deal!" Amanda said as she caught Sue's attention and placed her order.

"Why'd your dad want to get you away from your friends?" I queried while Amanda swirled hot fudge through the vanilla ice cream.

"He didn't like them."

"Why?"

"He said they were leading me down the wrong path, whatever that means. He just didn't understand."

Amanda offered me a bite of her sundae.

"Did they make you feel accepted?"

Amanda's big eyes opened wide.

"For sure, Vicki, I mean Victoria! For the first time in my life, I felt like I could be myself. People wanted to hang with me; you know, like I was popular."

"Did you tell that to your dad?"

"Yeah, but he wouldn't listen. He said they were a bunch of deadbeats who were druggies."

"Are they?"

"Some of them do drugs, some don't. I tried it once and got sick as a dog. I told them I wouldn't try it again. They respected me for who I am. My dad wouldn't even begin to get it."

Our waitress stopped by to give us the check. Amanda asked her if there was a restroom, and Sue pointed to the opposite side of the room. As she headed off, I paid our bill and left a tip. "Nice place," I added, picked up my purse, and decided I'd better stop by the restroom, too.

I had barely pushed the door open when I heard Amanda ask someone to lend her a phone. The woman was reaching into her pocketbook, but when Amanda saw me she said, "Never mind," and went into the cubicle.

After we washed up and got to the car, I said "So, that's what this was all about? You were walking into town to find a phone?"

Eyes to the ground, Amanda nodded. We got in the car and closed the doors.

"Here," I said, and handed her my phone. "Call Derek. If you tell him where you are, I'll grab it faster than you can say lickity split."

Where that expression came from, I'll never know. I sounded like Mary Poppins.

"Really?" she asked, grabbing the phone.

"Really."

I knew that both really's had different meanings, but I was serious. I didn't trust this Derek guy, I didn't want to jeopardize anyone at the monastery, and I certainly didn't want to incur the wrath of Sister Tony or the girl's father.

Amanda dialed. I could hear a girl's voice on the other end. "Hello?" Then in the background, I could hear a man's voice. "Give me the phone, sweetie. We got some more lovin' to do."

Amanda disconnected and handed me the phone, not saying a word. My heart sank for her, but my soul thanked the heavens for the divine intervention.

I stopped for gas as we headed back through town. I had no sooner swiped my credit card and put the nozzle in the gas tank when Amanda bolted from the car.

"Get back in the car, Amanda," I said firmly.

She looked at me with tears and mascara streaming down her cheeks, then turned and ran. A guy in the car behind me put down his window and said to me, "I've got a daughter just about her age, and let me tell you, it's not easy. Hormones! Geesh!"

"I know what you're saying," I said with a fake smile as I hung the nozzle back on its hook.

Amanda didn't get too far. I saw her sitting at a picnic table on the other side of the gas station. I pulled the car around, got out, and slowly joined her. She was sobbing. I had no words to say to stop the hurt that I knew Amanda was feeling. I put my hand on her shoulder, then sat next to her on the bench. I handed her some tissues from my purse, and she loudly blew her nose.

"I can't believe that sleezebag!" she yelled. "He was getting it on with my best friend! At least I thought she was my best friend! Who would do that? I thought Derek truly loved me...that's what he told me! I honestly believed him. And I loved him with all my heart!" Amanda let out a piercing wail and began to sob again.

The guy with the hormonal daughter pulled up and called out his window, "Is everything OK here?"

"We're fine," I replied. "Just a little spat."

"I hear you," he said as he pulled away. I had no doubt that he had experience with this type of thing, but I didn't.

"Men are jerks!" Amanda muttered as she blew her nose again. "Why didn't you say, 'I told you so'?"

"Because I didn't tell you so. And because I've been there. I lost the man I loved a long time ago, but I still remember the grief I felt."

Amanda nodded as if she recognized some sort of kindred connection with me, and we sat in silence.

After a while I said, "Shall we go back to the monastery?" She nodded again and we got into the car. I saw the tears that Amanda was brushing away, but knew that only time would help her to process the broken bubbles of her dreams.

As we pulled into the parking lot, Sister Tony was getting out of the golf cart.

"Where have you been, Amanda? I've been looking for you."

I interjected with an over-enthusiastic apology. "I'm so sorry, Sister. I invited Amanda to join me for lunch in town, and never thought to let you know."

She looked at Amanda's mascara-streaked face, then gazed at my expression. I'm sure it was evident to Sister Tony that something had upset Amanda.

"I'm afraid I hurt Amanda's feelings on our ride back to the monastery," I lied. "I told her that she needs to get rid of the neon hair and remove some of the jewelry if she ever hopes to get a job."

Tony looked at Amanda, who nodded in agreement, then back at me.

"Although I don't disagree, Victoria, that's a little harsh to say to someone you barely know, wouldn't you say?"

I agreed contritely.

"I'm sorry, Amanda. I'm accustomed to being rather direct, but I didn't mean to hurt your feelings."

"Apology accepted," she said with the hint of a smile, and I laughed.

"Private joke," I explained to Sister Tony.

"There, there, my dear. Come with me to the monastery, and you can get freshened up," she said gently as she led Amanda toward the monastery.

With particular conviction, she turned back to me and said, "Victoria, in the future, please inform me if you invite Amanda off the grounds."

"Yes, Sister," I promised.

Chapter 7

I carried our bag of goodies back to the cabin, planning to take Amanda's things to her cabin after supper. Betty was just stepping off my porch. Noting the bag, she said "Stir crazy already?" I laughed and told her that's just what Myra said when I informed her of my plans to go to go to town.

"I'm glad you stopped by," I said. "Want some iced tea? I'm parched."

Betty came with me into the kitchenette while I mixed up the powder and water in two glasses. I added a few mini ice cubes from the little freezer compartment of the refrigerator.

"I'm in big trouble. I lied to a nun."

"You're headed to perdition! Spill the beans."

I told her about my excursion and meeting Amanda on the road. When I got to the part about the phone, Betty exclaimed, "Oh, no!" and then a bigger "Oh, no!" about the heartbreaking response Amanda got.

"That poor child," Betty said. "What a sleazebag!"

"Yeah, she looked a mess when we pulled into the parking lot and met Sister Tony. Another "Oh, no!" came out of Betty's mouth. I explained that I had made up some flimsy excuse for Amanda's tears, and told Betty my lie.

"That's pretty lame. Did Tony buy it?"

"I think she did. She chastised me for being so callous. I felt like I was going to be sent to the principal's office."

"You took a big risk. If that creep Derek knew where Amanda was staying, he could have caused a lot of problems here, in addition to the anger you would have incurred with Amanda's father.

"I know. I don't know what made me hand that phone to her. I certainly didn't expect it to turn out the way it did."

"John and I had a similar situation one time. On one of our summer trips, we brought three boys from the city to the camp. Each one had his own issues, but Eugene was particularly insolent, feeling that his mother had forced him to go in order to get him away from his gang's influence."

"Had she?"

"In a way, yes. I was working with his mom, trying to get another hearing for her husband who was in jail for a robbery he said he hadn't committed. Anyway, we did everything we could to get Eugene involved at the campsite. When we swam at the lake, he sulked on the beach. If John or I would try to engage him in conversation, he either gave us the silent treatment, or barraged us with foul talk."

"After the third day, John drove Eugene back to the city, planning to arrive at his house about the same time his mother got home from work. John told me later that he didn't know what possessed him, but he stopped at the local street park where a lot of the gangs hang out, and told Eugene to get out of the car. Some of his buddies were playing basketball. Believe it or not, they turned on him, told him he'd been voted out. John had cruised around the block and returned just in time to see the ring leader punch Eugene in the face. John yelled, 'Police!' and they scattered, leaving Eugene with a bloody nose and no friends. He quietly got back in the car, and they returned to the camp."

"Wow. Lucky for Eugene that John got back when he did."

"I know. Later that night when we were out of earshot from the boys, I really gave it to John. We could laugh about it later, but I was so angry at the time."

"Did Eugene change his attitude?"

"Eventually. There must be some kind of silent honor system among the city kids because the other boys nonchalantly involved Eugene in their activities. The next day, they invited

Eugene to go fishing with them. John and I sat on the beach, watching them clown around on the boat. They didn't catch any fish that day, but when they returned to the dock, they were laughing and calling each other dorky names."

"Whatever happened to Eugene?"

"That's the best part. John got him into a program at the local community college, and Eugene eventually transferred to law school. He passed the bar, and now works for a city agency to advocate for needy families. He married a young woman he met at school, and they have two little boys."

"That's a great story."

Betty nodded thoughtfully. "Sometimes things happen for a reason that we don't comprehend at the moment. Maybe your intervention with Amanda will have a similar outcome. Maybe it won't. Time will tell. But I know this much. Amanda will never forget what you did for her today."

"And on that note," Betty added as she took her glass to the sink, "I'll leave you to your musings. Put something on that sunburn."

"I will," I laughed, showing her my purchases. I put on my visor and did a little "Ta da!"

"Oh, my goodness. You sure are a sight to see!"

^^^

After supper, I walked over to Amanda's cabin so I could drop off her baseball cap and goodies. She wasn't there. I was hesitant to leave them on the porch, envisioning some hungry bear feeding chips and candy to her cubs, but I was able to fit the bag inside the screen door. I hoped that Sister Tony was keeping watch over Amanda at the monastery. This was not a night for Amanda to be alone in a cabin.

As I returned to the path, I distinctly heard the sound of muffled crying in the woods. Thinking it may be Amanda, I pushed aside some saplings, and trudged through the underbrush. A woman was leaning into a tree, nestling her head in bent arms, her shoulders wracked with sobs. She turned toward me suddenly as she heard my foot crunch on a fallen branch. It was obvious that I had startled her.

"I'm so sorry. I didn't mean to intrude," and began to back away.

"I've seen you before. You're in one of the cabins."

"I'm Victoria. Are you OK?"

"No, I'm Maggie. I mean my name is Maggie," she stammered. I didn't think she was trying to make a joke. "I don't know what came over me, but it's like that a lot lately. I feel fine, and then I just burst into tears."

I nodded, like I understood. There seems to be a lot of crying going around today.

"Maybe it's not so good for you to be alone right now."

"I have a lot to work through," Maggie said, stifling a sob. She took a deep breath. "I need to be alone right now."

"I'm sorry," I repeated and turned to retreat.

"No, wait, I didn't mean at this minute. I meant right now."

I stopped, wondering what in the world she was talking about. I faced her again. Maggie was tall and slender, and looked to be in her mid- to late-30's. She had long brown hair pulled back into a pony tail, and wore shorts and a t-shirt. This must be the gal Betty had mentioned.

"Do you want to talk?" I asked.

She nodded and said, "Do you mind coming to my cabin? I need to get some tissues."

I agreed and followed her. She seemed to know her way through the trees. I sat on one of the rocking chairs and said, "You go freshen up and I'll wait here for you."

A few minutes later she came out with two cans of cold soda and handed me one. I opened mine and took a swig. I didn't quite know what to say.

"I left my husband," she said abruptly. A tear was trying to escape, but she quickly brushed it away.

I still didn't know what to say, but I faltered, "And was that a good thing?"

"I don't know. That's why I came here. You know, to think about it. The problem is, I don't know what to do. My week is over in two days, and I'm not ready to go back home yet. Sister Tony said I could stay a few more days, if I wanted. The next reservation cancelled at the last moment. I called Ted—that's my husband—to tell him, and he didn't even pick up my call. I finally just hung up."

"So, this was only a temporary arrangement?"

"Yeah, but I can't stand to be around him. All we do is fight. Rather, I fight and he gives me the silent treatment. He buries himself in work, or goes to his man cave watching sports. I finally had enough and told him I needed a week away. I thought this might be a good place when I saw the brochure. My sister lives in South Carolina and she wanted me to visit her, but I just wanted time to think it all out alone. She doesn't know it's as bad as it is."

"How long have you been married?"

"Ten years. It'll be eleven years in August. At first it was great. We both had good jobs in advertising, but I wanted to start a family. When I didn't get pregnant right away, I figured I had plenty of time. Then, two years ago I realized that time was ticking away. I quit my job and began rounds of *in vitro* fertilization. Ted was supportive at first, but our savings were dwindling, and one pay check didn't get us through the month. That's when we started arguing. It infuriates me when he just walks away."

"Maybe you could see a marriage counselor."

"Ted said that, too, but I know we don't have the money, and I really don't know if I want to try any more. I'd be better off on my own."

I knew this was not the time to add my two cents, so I just listened.

"Anyway, I told Sister Tony that I was staying. Ted obviously didn't have anything to say to me, so I doubt that it matters to him."

"Maybe he was in a meeting or something when you called."

"I don't care. I'm going to take as much time as I want to figure out what to do."

Dusk was falling, and Maggie seemed to be more settled.

"Will you be OK if I leave now?"

Maggie nodded. "I actually feel better since I talked to you. I hadn't told anyone about what I was feeling. My friends knew something was wrong, but I didn't want to unload on them. They all have their own problems."

"I know, but sometimes expressing our inner thoughts, you know, putting words to them, helps to clarify our emotions." Maggie nodded in agreement.

"I'm in the end cabin," I said, "and I'll be here for a few more days. Stop by any time if you want to chat."

Maggie looked at me, and smiled for the first time.

"Thank you. You have no idea how much you helped me tonight."

Chapter 8

I checked my messages in the morning and returned a few business calls. There was nothing critical, and I was able to tie up loose ends rather quickly. I began to write out my schedule.

Despite a good night's sleep, I was still a little tired from the day before. I knew better than to get bogged down with other people's troubles, but I couldn't help mulling over yesterday's conversations. I really hadn't given much thought about my own future, I realized, but somehow that didn't seem so important when I saw the difficult challenges facing my new acquaintances.

I decided to pop by to see if Maggie wanted to explore the lake with me. She was sitting on her front porch, engrossed in a novel.

"Is it any good?" I asked, startling her. She recovered quickly.

"Actually, it is. But I'm glad you stopped by."

"I'm on my way to the lake. Would you like to join me?" Maggie seemed to hesitate.

"I'd like some company," I said. I can connive with the best of them.

Noticing the towel and visor in my hand, Maggie said, "I'll get something to sit on. But I'm not wearing one of those things." We both laughed.

"Visors are the latest trend in designer fashion. You'll be sorry when I'm selected for the cover of Vogue."

When we got to the lake, I saw Charlie fishing on the anchored raft and Betty sitting on the beach. Maggie seemed reluctant to continue, but I urged her forward saying, "Oh, look! There's Betty. You'll like her." Betty looked toward my voice and waved.

"Her highness, Princess Victoria, and her jeweled crown," intoned Betty.

"One more blasted comment about my new hat, and I'll throw you both in the brink. Betty, this is Maggie. Maggie, Betty."

As I knew she would, Betty extended a warm welcome.

"You flirting with Charlie?" I teased Betty. She rolled her eyes and laughed.

"Don't give me that look, missy!" I chastised in mock horror. "I met Charlie the other evening, and he's quite a nice gentleman."

"No way! Did he actually talk?"

"Yep. He said, 'I'd best be on my way.'" Betty burst out laughing, while Maggie looked at me quizzically.

I explained that the guy fishing on the raft was known to be a man of few words, and that he lived in the farthest cabin. Maggie noted that she had seen him pulling weeds from the flower beds along the main drive.

"Right," I said. "That's how he got started here about ten years ago. That, and doing odd jobs."

I explained that Charlie often brought fish from the lake to the Sisters, and distributed produce to local shelters on Tuesdays. I added that he had designed the cabins, and it was his idea for the poustinia business. Betty sat with her mouth open.

"Well, for a new-comer, you sure do get around."

I gave her a triumphant look. "I guess I do, Miss Betty. I guess I do."

"How long have you two known each other?" Maggie asked.

"Three days," Betty said. "We just seemed to hit it off right away. Guess I have a new friend. By the way, have you seen Amanda today?

"Who's Amanda?" Maggie asked.

"She's the kid in the cabin next to mine."

Maggie nodded, like she knew whom we were speaking about.

"No, I haven't seen her today," I said. "I'm hoping she stayed at the monastery last night after our encounter with Sr. Tony. Have you seen her?"

"No, but you're probably right." We watched a few birds pecking at the beach.

Betty turned to Maggie. "So, you're here for a little alone-time?"

Maggie seemed startled. "What makes you say that?" she replied defensively.

Betty responded with a chuckle, "Because that's what we're all here for, in one way or another, although Victoria hasn't really told us why she's here."

"I'm here for a little alone-time."

"And...?" Betty prompted.

"And nothing else." After a moment or two, I added, "I want to figure out what I want to do in my senior years."

"Get out of here. You're not old!" Betty exclaimed.

"That's what you say because you're about the same age that I am. Seriously, I've been thinking I want to move out of the corporate world while I'm at the top, not after I lose my edge. I'm just not sure what I want to do, or how I'd go about it."

"It's probably something we all wrestle with from time to time," Betty said. "I have to admit, though, I love my advocacy work, and I don't think I'll ever leave it."

Maggie said, "I was in advertising before I took some time off, but I think I want to start job hunting again soon. I still dabble with photography and building websites, and I'm still current with technology. I know I want to stay in the field."

"Why'd you take time off?" Betty asked.

"I wanted to start a family, but it didn't happen."

"Same with me."

"Really? Did you ever get pregnant?"

"No. It was a rough patch in our marriage, but John and I worked it out, and we started helping kids in the city."

I was happy that Maggie was opening up to Betty. I had a good feeling about the way this conversation was headed.

Maggie looked down to the sand and pebbles.

"I don't think we can work this out. My marriage is beyond repair."

"Are you abused?"

"Oh, no! Nothing like that! We just can't communicate any more. I yell; he gets silent. It's just not working."

"It's not working because you're both confused and hurting in your own way. And you're grieving. Of course you can't communicate right now. But, I think you've taken a big first step by coming here to think it out."

"I came here to get away from Ted."

"Maybe on the surface," Betty said. "A cat hides behind a chair and sleeps when it needs to get better; a dog lies in the corner, licking his paws. Think of your stay here as a time to lick your paws." I had to admit, Betty made a lot of sense.

"We don't know what the future holds for any of us," Betty added. "What we do know is that we can develop resiliency and strength as we face life's curve balls. Yours is a tough one, I know. But don't close your mind and heart to great possibilities."

In the distance, we saw Charlie stand and stretch, then move to the far side of the platform. We watched as he eased himself off the raft and into the water.

"I don't know how he can stand that cold water," I said.

All of the sudden, Betty exclaimed, "He's got a canoe! Look at that! All this time I thought he swam out there, but he ties a canoe to the other side of the raft!"

Charlie paddled to the shore, jumped out, and pulled the canoe onto the beach about 100 yards from where we sat. He held a line with two nice sized fish attached and walked toward the woods.

"'Morning, ladies," he nodded as he passed by.

"You got a new boat, Charlie?"

"One of the new additions around here. Anyone can use it."

"Nice," Betty said. "Really nice! Who's up for a canoe ride?"

"I'm game," Maggie replied.

"Not me. I've had enough sun for the day. You two can test it out."

Despite their protests, I shook out my towel, then watched as they dragged the canoe into the lake. Betty got in and steadied the canoe as Maggie stepped in. I could hear their giggles as I trudged towards the trees.

^^^

I stopped at Amanda's cabin on my way back, but she wasn't there, and the bag was still between the doors. After a light lunch, I decided to walk to the monastery, and check to see if Amanda was OK.

Sister Tony opened the massive door shortly after I rang the bell. "Good afternoon, Victoria. Won't you come in?"

I explained that I was concerned because Amanda hadn't been to her cabin.

"That's kind of you, dear. I thought it might be best if Amanda stayed with us last night."

"I was hoping you'd say that." I sighed with relief as I followed Tony to her office.

"Have a seat, Victoria. I think I was a little harsh with you yesterday, and I apologize. I appreciate that you've gone out of your way to watch over Amanda. She told me that you comforted her during the storm the other night."

"I think we helped each other. That was a doozy."

"It was. At least I heard it was from some of the Sisters. I slept right through it. Nonetheless, I should have listened to my gut feeling when the girl's father requested that she stay for the week. He said Amanda was a tough cookie and would have no problem staying alone."

"She puts on a rough exterior, but she's a lonely child within. The neon hair and piercings are more like a cry for attention."

"I agree, which is why I don't think you'd make a brash statement to Amanda. Why was she crying, Victoria? She hasn't eaten a thing, and she isn't speaking to any of us."

"You're right. But I don't want to betray Amanda's confidence. Why don't we see if I can get her to open up to you."

"I believe she's on the veranda. I'll take you there."

I followed Sister Tony past the grand staircase and down a long hallway with beautiful mahogany wainscoting and parlors on both sides. There was an elevator straight ahead, and I noticed a corridor to the right and to the left.

Tony pointed to the left side and said, "That's our refectory. It's what we call our dining room. In the old days, we used to have one long table; now it's more restaurant style dining. A large industrial kitchen is located behind the double doors."

We took the right hallway, then passed some offices and parlors. "Our chapel is straight ahead, and on our left is the community room," Tony noted as she ushered me into the large living area. The room was attractively decorated with various sitting areas, coffee tables, and a large-screen TV in the corner. French doors led to a screened-in porch with a variety of wicker furniture.

Amanda sat by herself in the far corner, deep in thought. She seemed smaller than ever, all scrunched up, leaning on one of the massive arm rests.

"Victoria's here to see you, Amanda."

Amanda looked up at me, those big brown eyes seeming to shimmer. There was no mascara today, and it added to her beauty.

"Hey, Amanda. I brought your stuff to your cabin, but you weren't there, so I came looking for you." No response.

I turned to Tony. "We both got hats yesterday. Amanda made fun of mine." I saw the faintest tweak of a smile out of the corner of my eyes.

"Just don't wear it in public," Amanda said softly.

"Too late. The other folks around here agree with you."

"May we sit down?" I asked.

She nodded her approval.

"Sister Tony's worried about you. Do you want to tell her about yesterday?"

Amanda shook her head to indicate that she didn't want to talk about it.

"You won't get me in trouble, I promise. Besides, I pride myself on the highest of ethics, and I didn't tell Sister Tony the truth."

"I was walking into town," Amanda replied after some hesitation, watching for a response on Tony's face. Seeing none, she continued. "Vicki, I mean Victoria, picked me up and we bought hats and stuff at the drug store, and then we went to lunch. It was fun." She looked at me and smiled.

"That was nice, Amanda," Tony said, "but why were you walking to town? One of the Sisters would have been glad to take you."

Silence. I nodded slowly towards Amanda, begging her with my eyes to go on.

"I needed to find a phone to call my friends."

Tony exhaled slowly. "Oh, I see," she said cautiously.

"No, you don't see! No one sees! My dad took away my phone and left me here alone. I might as well be dead for all he cares!"

"He loves you very much, Amanda," Tony said softly. "He was frightened about the influences you were facing."

"There's more," I added. Amanda closed her eyes and took a deep breath.

"Victoria let me use her phone to call Derek."

Tony looked at me, but her face was expressionless. "And..."

"And, he was getting it on with my best friend!" Amanda put her head in her arms and sobbed.

Tony went over and put her hand on Amanda's shoulder. "Do you want to go home?"

"I don't know what to do. I don't want to see my father, I don't want to see Derek, and I don't want to see my friends ever again!"

I thought of Betty's analogy of licking one's paws.

"I think you'll want to see your dad and your friends again. You just need time to process what you've been through. It's a rite of passage, Amanda."

"I have an idea," I said. "I'll be leaving in a day or two. Maybe we could convince your dad to let you visit me for a few weeks."

Amanda looked up in surprise. So did Tony. Where the heck that came from, I have no idea. I just had a feeling that Amanda needed some attention, not time alone in a cabin, and certainly not back with her so-called friends.

Amanda looked up with wide eyes. "Are you serious?" Tony said the same thing almost simultaneously.

"I am. I haven't thought through the details, but I am serious."

"Don't you work full time?" Tony asked.

"I do. That's the part we need to figure out. Maybe Amanda and I could brainstorm the possibilities this afternoon, and then touch base with you this evening."

"We'd have to contact Amanda's father."

"Of course, but not until we have a concrete plan. He'll probably also want to look into my background and, perhaps, check out my firm's website. I'd also be perfectly happy to meet with him and discuss this in person."

Tony felt that Amanda should return to spend another night at the monastery, and I concurred. Amanda didn't want to stay alone in the cabin, so we planned that Tony would come for her in the golf cart after she and I had supper at my place. Then they could stop by Amanda's cabin and pick up a change of clothing and some toiletries.

Chapter 9

Amanda and I left the monastery, both of us enveloped in our thoughts as we walked to my cabin. I went in and got each of us a cold beverage, while Amanda sat on the porch. I handed her a glass of iced tea and sat down in the other rocking chair.

"How old are you, Amanda?"

"I'm 18."

"Did you complete high school?"

"Yeah, I graduated in June. I didn't do great last year, but I passed."

I didn't want it to sound like I was grilling her, so I asked her to tell me about some of the subjects she liked best. She mentioned that she liked English, especially literature, but she wasn't so crazy about math and science. She had also taken a cooking class and enjoyed that.

"What does this have to do with our plan?"

"Not much. I just wanted to know more about you."

"So, how old are you and what do you do?"

"I'm 61 and executive Vice President of Human Resources for a publishing firm. I'm single, own a 3-bedroom, 2-bath home in the suburbs, and you know about Harvey." Amanda seemed satisfied that we were on equal playing fields.

"I have plenty of room for you to stay. You could have the guest room and bath. And Harvey sure would like the company. You're not allergic to dogs, are you?"

"No, I love dogs. I've been trying to convince Dad to get one, but he didn't want the hassle, whatever that means."

"My biggest concern is that it would be boring for you. There aren't many kids in the neighborhood, and you'd be home alone all day." I was still mulling that dilemma when Amanda suggested that she could come to work with me.

"I don't think... Wait a minute! You may be onto something!"

I suddenly remembered that we were advertising for a temporary entry level office assistant. Amanda met the criteria, and her interest in books was a plus.

"Let me get my phone."

I called into the office and learned that no one had yet been hired for the position, although some ranking of candidates had been completed. After a little debriefing and tying up some loose ends, I disconnected and told Amanda about the job.

"Wow! Do you think I'd qualify?"

"I don't see why not. One of the department secretaries is on maternity leave and, while the others are all picking up the slack, they need a temp to do odd jobs. I could help you with a resume if you don't have one. I think we have the beginning of our plan!"

We spent the next two hours outlining the specifics and building Amanda's resume. We figured that Tony would let Amanda use her computer this evening, and help her fax a cover letter and resume in the morning. Then, we'd call her dad. If he gave his approval, we'd stop at her house the day after next, so she could gather some appropriate attire, then head to my place.

Finally, we went in and foraged through the last remaining bags of groceries I had brought to make some supper. We had barely finished cleaning up when Betty appeared at the door.

"We have some exciting news," I announced.

Amanda told Betty about what had transpired. With that, Tony rounded the bend, and Amanda gathered her papers. Amanda hopped into the passenger side of the golf cart. I could see her talking a mile a minute as Tony drove to Amanda's cabin.

"I'm proud of you," Betty said. "That girl needs a positive influence, and you stepped up to the plate."

"I don't think I'd ever have thought of it had you not told me about the kids that you and John helped. In fact, I hadn't even mulled about it. The idea just popped into my head, and then it took shape."

"It won't be easy. Amanda seems to have a lot of baggage that she has to work through, from what you've told me. You'll have to deal with the emotions from the scumbag boyfriend and the loss of her so-called friends. On top of that, you have no experience working with a teen who has so many issues. Have you really thought it through?"

"Probably not as much as I should. I have experience with young people I've hired for the firm. Granted, I don't deal with their personal problems, but I'm a good listener, and I've helped many of them to rise through the ranks. I'm pretty good with finding the strengths in others, and I see many positive assets in Amanda. Are you thinking I'm crazy?"

"No, I don't think you're crazy. I think Amanda's lucky that she ran to your cabin when she was frightened in the storm. What does her father think about this scheme of yours?"

"We haven't asked him yet. I wanted a firm plan in place before we approached him."

"Amanda's going to be mighty upset if he doesn't approve."

"That's true, but I feel certain he'll approve. Think about it. He doesn't know what to do with his young adult daughter, and he wants her away from bad influences. She obviously can't be sent to a monastery for the rest of her life. I think Tony will put in a good word for me, even though she's only known me for a short time. It's a win-win for Amanda and her dad."

"I just hope it's a win-win for you and Amanda. Regardless, I'm proud of you!"

"So, how was your canoe ride with Maggie?" I asked, changing the subject.

"It was fun! Maggie and I took turns paddling all around the lake, although we almost turned over a few times. I should have borrowed your visor," she said, touching her red nose.

"Did you two talk more about what Maggie was going through?"

"A little. But, more importantly, we just had fun. I think it helped Maggie relax and stop dwelling on the hurt she's been feeling. I'll tell you, that canoe is a nice addition to the lake. I got a great workout, and I was surprised that I remembered all the skills that John showed me when we'd go camping.

"A canoe can be a little tricky to maneuver. I tried it years ago and capsized just trying to get settled in the seat."

"I know what you mean. Maggie and I seemed able to balance pretty well. It's kind of like life, in a manner of speaking, don't you think? If things get thrown off kilter, we either over-compensate, or we get submerged. Two people make it even more difficult. Maggie and Ted are in that boat right now. It's wobbling all over the place and, unless they both settle in and balance themselves, they're going to go under."

"Do you think they'll be able to work it out?"

"It's too early to say. It's going to take both of them to fix it; both of them paddling in the same direction. I'm keeping my fingers crossed. And, on that note, I wanted to remind you that I'll be leaving in the morning. I'm going to head back to my cabin to pack my stuff and get a good night's sleep. Keep me posted and let me know how it works out with Amanda."

"I'm so happy that we met up this week. I really enjoyed your company."

"Likewise," Betty agreed. We exchanged phone numbers, and I gave her a hug to send her on her way.

Chapter 10

In the morning, I trekked to the monastery and met with Sister Tony and Amanda. We insisted that Amanda be the one to call her dad, but assured her that we'd be there for support and, if she wanted, to back her up using the speaker phone. Notes in hand, Amanda practiced her speech ahead of time, then dialed the number.

Amanda's father listened, but was hesitant. Sensing that Amanda was about to go into her attitude mode, I signaled for her to bring us into the conversation.

"Hello, Mr. Angeli. This is Victoria Sullivan, and Sister Antoinette is here with me."

We spent about 25 minutes reviewing the plan, and it wasn't an easy sell. In the end, Mr. Angeli agreed to think about it, and let us know his decision.

"Give me an hour and I'll call you back," he said.

I figured he'd do a background check on me, as I would do if I were wearing his shoes. Amanda was pacing while I read through the resume she had typed. It was actually well constructed and attractively designed. Tony was impressed as well, noting that Amanda had spent hours on the computer the night before.

"I'd say it's ready to go as soon as we get your dad's approval." Amanda beamed.

The three of us were startled with the chimes of the front doorbell. Tony excused herself to answer the door. She returned to say that she needed to take someone to a cabin and would be right back.

While we waited, Amanda and I began to discuss the difference between professional dress and business casual. She admitted that most of her wardrobe consisted of jeans, shorts, and skimpy tops. She'd definitely need some new attire. I suggested that we not count our eggs before they hatched, reminding her that this was a difficult decision for her father.

When the phone rang, we both jumped. I decided to answer it.

"Good morning, Monastery of St. Carmella," I said in my most professional voice.

"Good morning. This is Steve Angeli. May I speak to my daughter?"

"Certainly. She's right here."

I handed the phone to Amanda. I knew the outcome by the excited squeals of joy, with a dozen thank you's interspersed. Amanda handed the phone to me so that her dad and I could make final arrangements to meet the next day.

Sister Tony returned as I disconnected, and Amanda quickly filled in the details of our conversation. While Amanda was busy trying to send her paperwork through the fax with the number I provided, Tony turned to me and said, "I hope I did the right thing."

I gave her a questioning look. "I know in my heart it's the right thing."

"No, not you and Amanda. The reason I took so long was because I brought a gentleman to see his wife in one of the cabins."

"Ted came to see Maggie?"

"You know about them?"

I explained about my encounter with Maggie in the woods, and then our enjoyable afternoon at the lake yesterday. "Nice canoe, by the way."

"Yes, we received a sizable donation. Charlie convinced me that it would be put to good use."

"So, what happened when you got to Maggie's cabin?"

"It was actually sweet. Maggie cried, and I left them kissing on the porch. I just hope I didn't open a can of worms."

"What's sweet?" Amanda inquired as she returned with the notification that her fax had been successfully sent.

"You are. Now, how about if you and I go out to lunch and do some clothes shopping. I hear there's an outlet mall not too far from here."

Tony laughed, and agreed that was a good idea. She reminded Amanda that her dad had left some money in case she needed anything.

"Now *that's* sweet!" Amanda exclaimed.

We gathered all of Amanda's papers as Tony retrieved $200 from her locked desk drawer. She gave us directions, and I assured her that we'd return by nightfall. Amanda practically skipped to the car.

^^^

Amanda wanted to give a fashion show to the Sisters when we returned and, despite my protests, she lugged every one of her purchases from the car. Tony laughed when she opened the door, but encouraged Amanda to go upstairs and show her wares to the Sisters. As she departed toward the elevator, I told Tony that we'd be leaving the next afternoon, with enough time to coordinate my meeting with Amanda's father, and to give Amanda an opportunity to gather some things from home. I left my car keys with Tony so Amanda could pack the trunk in the morning.

"Any news on the cabin front?" I asked.

"Well, Betty left today... and Maggie and Ted went out to dinner. She called our phone line to say that Ted would be staying a few days with her."

"Nice!"

"I hope so. Time will tell."

By the time I got back to the cabin, dusk was approaching, and I was really tired. I thought I had better give Myra a quick call to remind her that I was returning the next evening, and that Amanda would be joining me.

"Are you going kookie? First you go off to some God-forsaken place in the woods, and now you're bringing home some waif you hardly know!" I could see her shaking her head in disdain.

"It's really not as bad as you're imagining." I explained that we would first be stopping at Amanda's home, and then had another hour's drive.

"Come on over whenever you get back," Myra said. "I'm sure I'll still be up, and Harvey will be happy that you're home."

I locked up and went to bed, figuring I'd pack in the morning. I think I was asleep before my head hit the pillow.

Chapter 11

In the morning, I took one last trek to the lake. It was a beautiful day, but the air had a sultry feel, and a mist clung to the trees. It seemed to portend a hot, hazy afternoon and, probably, evening storms. I noticed the canoe was not on the beach, and expected to see Charlie fishing at his usual spot with the boat harnessed to the raft. No Charlie.

My eyes gazed across the shimmering water and, in the distance, I saw Maggie and Ted paddling the canoe—perfectly balanced and in unity. I smiled.

Amanda and I departed exactly the time we had planned, so that we'd arrive at Amanda's house when her dad would be home. Tony waved us off, and reminded us to return soon. Amanda seemed to be a kettle of mixed emotions. We were barely on the main road before she said, "Don't tell my dad about Derek."

"I wasn't planning to do that. It seems to me that's something you're going to want to do when you're ready."

"I'm not going to tell him. He'd just say, 'I told you so.'"

I glanced over to see a very determined look on Amanda's face.

"There's no reason for the topic to even come up in conversation today. But, if it did, all you need to say is that you're taking some time away from Derek so that you can explore this new opportunity. End of story."

"Yeah, that could work. I'm still really angry with him."

"Who? Derek or your dad?"

"I was talking about Derek, but I could also include my dad because he caused the whole problem in the first place."

"I can see how you might think that, but regardless of what triggered the event, a man of honor doesn't betray his commitment to another person. Your dad kept his side of the fatherhood deal by trying to protect his daughter from any real or imagined danger."

"It doesn't matter. I'm still kind of mad at him, but at least he's letting me stay with you for a few weeks."

"I imagine that was a difficult decision for him."

"I don't want to talk about it anymore."

Amanda fiddled with the radio dial to find a station with her kind of music.

^^^

Amanda's dad came out to meet us when we pulled into her driveway. Amanda introduced us, then announced that she had to gather some of her things from the house before her dad had a chance to welcome her home.

As she ran off, he stood on the walkway shaking his head as if he didn't know what to do. Suddenly, he said, "Where are my manners? Please come in. There's a powder room half way down the hall on the left. I have some iced tea ready in the kitchen."

When I settled myself at the kitchen table, Mr. Angeli asked me more questions about why I had invited Amanda to my home. I told him about the storm on my first night at the cabin, and how Amanda and I comforted each other.

"Amanda never did like storms. I hadn't thought about how she'd react to a storm when she was alone in a cabin."

"Well, I was grateful to have someone with me. It was my first time alone in the woods, and I was a little nervous myself. Anyway, I saw that Amanda has some real strengths, and I wanted to give her an opportunity at my firm."

I left out some key details, but Steve Angeli seemed satisfied.

We heard the clunk of a large suitcase as Amanda dragged it down the stairs. She popped her head into the kitchen and said, "OK, I'm ready. Let's go!"

"Don't you want any iced tea, honey?"

"Nah, I'm good. Thanks anyway, Dad. We want to get to Victoria's place before dark."

All in all, my meeting with Amanda's father went well, and I liked him. He thanked me for giving this opportunity to his daughter. I could see that he really didn't quite know how to handle a young woman struggling to find her identity. As we prepared to leave, he gave Amanda some spending money, and reminded her to follow my house rules. I left my address and phone numbers.

"Can I have my phone back?"

"Not until you earn it."

As we drove away, I could tell that Amanda was annoyed about the phone thing, so I tried to get her talking.

"Tell me about your mom. Did she have any hobbies?"

Amanda replied that her mother loved to draw and paint. "Even when I was little, I remember her always carrying a sketch pad in her purse. If we went to the park, she'd draw me playing on the swings or in the sandbox. She had an awesome way of adding details that most people don't notice in their surroundings. On Sunday afternoons, she'd set up her easel and paint scenes from her sketches. They were really cool."

"Did you inherit any of her talent?"

"Nah, not really. I'd sit at a desk and color some of her sketches when she was painting, but when I tried to draw, nothing came out right. Dad always said I took after him in that department. I do think my mom taught me a lot about design, like putting together different colors and textures. It's kind of neat."

"That's a great knack. I like watching those design shows on TV, and I'm always amazed at what they accomplish in a home makeover. I wouldn't know where to start!"

We both laughed, and I could see that Amanda was beginning to relax a bit.

"Mom liked those shows, too.   When she got sick, sometimes I'd snuggle up with her on the sofa, and we'd talk about what designs she liked, and what ones she thought needed to be changed."

"How old were you when she got sick?"

"I was 12 when she was first diagnosed with cancer. I remember coming home from school—I was in 7th grade—and she cried when she told me. It made me scared because my 4th grade teacher got cancer, and she died when I was in 5th grade. Anyway, when dad got home from work, we had a family meeting and discussed mom's treatment options.   She had radiation and chemotherapy. That made her really sick, and she lost all her hair."

"I'm sure that was difficult for her."

"It was. Mom had really pretty hair. She got a wig for when she went out, but at home she'd just go bald. When her hair started to grow back in after the chemo, it was the strangest thing because she had curls she'd never had before."

"I've heard that happens sometimes."

"Things were going great for a while. Then, just as I was beginning my junior year in high school, mom's cancer came back. This time it went to her bones and liver. She died in early December that year."

We both sat quietly for a while. "Is your mother still alive?" Amanda asked.

"No. My mom died of cancer, too. I was a lot older than you when it happened, but it's a great loss when our mothers die. My dad died last year. He had retired in Florida, and enjoyed golfing with his buddies. He seemed to be doing great, even had a lady friend, but he suddenly keeled over with a massive heart attack on the 4th green last September."

"Bummer! That must have been a shock."

"It was. It hit me hard, but I found strength knowing that he'd lived a full life and, after 88 years, died doing what he loved to do."

I noticed we were only about ten miles from home. "Do me a favor, Amanda," I said. "Take my phone and search in my contacts for Bella's Pizza. Do you like pepperoni?"

Amanda nodded as she reached for my phone.

"Good," I said. "Order a large pepperoni and say we'll pick it up in about 15 minutes." When we reached the pizzeria, I handed Amanda a twenty, and she ran in to get it.

^^^

It wasn't quite dark when we unpacked the car, and put the pizza on the kitchen counter. "Do you want to come with me to get Harvey?"

Amanda said she wanted to meet Myra, so we walked next door and rang the front bell. I heard Harvey barking up a storm in the background.

Myra answered the door and said, "I saw you pull into the driveway. Welcome home! And, this must be Amanda. Come on in."

We did the round of introductions, and Amanda seemed pleased that Myra knew her by name. Myra appeared to focus on Amanda's neon hair and piercings, but she was wise enough not to say anything.

Myra invited us to sit and have a cup of tea, but I knew we were intruding on her evening TV shows. I begged off saying that we had a warm pizza waiting for us. Harvey seemed to take to Amanda right away, and was eager to let Amanda put him on his leash. I gathered his things and told Myra that we'd catch up after work the next day.

Amanda and I were both hungry, and we polished off the pizza in no time. After cleaning up, I showed Amanda to her room, and helped her lug in her bags. I retrieved a clean towel and wash cloth from the hall closet, and told Amanda to make herself at home. Finally, I gave the grand tour, with Harvey lapping at our heels, and offered to help Amanda unpack.

"That's OK. I can do it later. Do you know if I have the job?"

"Nothing's been decided yet. The team would like to interview you tomorrow, so I thought you might want to go to work with me in the morning. I leave at 7:45 a.m. Think you can be ready?"

"Sure!"

"Great. Breakfast is at 7:15."

I left her wrestling with Harvey on the floor.

"Did you hear that, Harvey?" I heard Amanda saying as I left to do a load of laundry. "We get up mighty early around here."

Chapter 12

A manda was right on time in the morning, and looked very nice in one of her new outfits. As we drank our tea, I prepared some toast and jelly, and reminded myself that I needed to get some fresh milk and bananas for my usual cereal in the morning.

I noticed that Amanda had on a little lipstick and eye shadow, but no dark eyeliner or mascara. Something else was different. I stared at her intently.

"What?" she questioned.

I realized that Amanda had removed her nose and tongue jewelry.

"Nothing. I was just thinking how pretty you look." She rolled her eyes.

When we arrived at the firm, I showed Amanda my office in Human Resources. Marge said that she had set up the interviews, and would have Amanda complete the required paperwork. I told Amanda that I'd meet her for lunch at noon, but if she finished earlier than that, she could come to my office.

At 11:45 a.m., I looked up to see Amanda at my door. I couldn't read her expression, so I said, "Well?" She practically danced into the room singing, "I got the job! And I start this afternoon!"

Over lunch, Amanda told me all about her interviews. The time passed quickly and we scurried to get back so she wouldn't be late. We agreed to meet at my office at 5 p.m.

On the way home, Amanda chatted about her orientation, and some of the activities she had completed during her first afternoon on the job. We stopped at the grocery store to get some items for dinner and breakfast, and decided to celebrate with grilled steak and corn on the cob.

I set the table, while Amanda called her father with the good news. After supper, we took Harvey for a walk around the block, with a final stop at Myra's. She was sitting on the front porch, reading the paper.

Amanda told Myra about the day's events, describing in detail her job responsibilities and the people she worked with. Myra appropriately responded at all the right places, though she could barely get in a word.

Harvey was getting restless, so Amanda suggested that she take Harvey home and play ball with him in the yard. I agreed, saying that I'd be home shortly.

As she left, Myra commented that she could see why I wanted to rescue Amanda.

"Oh, my. You'd think I found her at the pound."

"I didn't mean it that way."

"I know. Amanda's been through a lot and just needed some direction. But she's strong, smart, and resilient. I think she's going to be fine."

"It's not going to be easy, you know. You don't have a lot of experience with teenagers. They can be a little hormonal."

"I've discovered that already. But I'm going to just be myself, and I'll try to give her the space to be herself. She's a young woman, not a child."

I told Myra about meeting Betty at the monastery, and how inspirational she is in helping others, especially struggling families.

"Is she a nun?"

"No. She's a lawyer and works in advocacy. Her husband died suddenly a few years ago, and she goes to the poustinias to relax and unwind. She said it kind of reminds her of a camp that she and her husband used to go to, and they even brought kids from the city for weekend getaways."

"She sounds like a good person."

"I like her. She's about my age, and we really hit it off. I feel like I made a new friend. Anyway, I think she'll be able to give me good advice if I run into any snags with Amanda. Plus, you've raised your family and now have grandchildren. I can rely on your wisdom."

"I don't know if I'd call it wisdom, but I have lots of experience. You know, one of my granddaughters is about Amanda's age. She got a summer job, and she's going to culinary school in the fall. Maybe I could invite her for a weekend, and she could introduce Amanda to some of her friends. You've met her, Michael's youngest, Kate."

"Kate's a sweetheart. I forgot that she graduated in June. Amanda told me she likes to cook, so they might have something in common."

Myra and I chatted a little while longer, and I returned to the house as the orange glow of the sun slipped below the horizon. Amanda had turned on the lamps and television, and was relaxing on the sofa with Harvey's muzzle on her lap. Now that's a portrait Amanda's mother would have enjoyed painting, I thought, as I joined them to watch TV.

"You know," I said during one of the commercials, "this weekend is the 4th of July. I think we ought to have a cookout, and go to the fireworks display in town. What do you think?"

"Sure, whatever. Do you have any munchies?"

"We forgot to buy some. There are probably some crackers in the kitchen cabinet. Check it out, and see what you can find."

Amanda returned with a napkin full of crackers, each spread with a dollop of grape jelly, put them on her lap, and immersed herself in the show.

"Did you make one for me?"

"I didn't know you wanted one. I'll make you some at the next commercial."

Clearly, we were going to need to fine-tune the niceties of sharing our space.

"That's OK. I'm going to do a little reading and hit the sack early tonight. Would you let Harvey out, and lock up before you go to bed?"

"No problem."

I gave Harvey a little belly rub before heading to my room. The mutt seemed to like his new friend, and didn't even follow me down the hallway.

^^^

On the drive to work the next day, I once again brought up my idea of celebrating the 4th of July. Amanda still didn't seem too enthused, but she was more responsive.

"If you want to have a cookout, that's OK with me, but don't you think fireworks are a little dorky?"

"What's dorky about fireworks?"

"My friends call them the 'bombs of the establishment.'"

I glanced over and saw that she was looking out the passenger side window.

"Didn't you ever go to a fireworks display when you were a kid?"

"I don't think so. Not a real live one. My mom used to like to watch fireworks on TV, like the kind that has an orchestra playing to cover up the noise of the explosions. That was cool."

I realized that Amanda's fear of storms was probably related to the sound of the thunder, and fireworks were also scary to her.

"Well, we don't have to go to the fireworks display in town," I said. "We can just watch the special on TV. I think I'd like that better, too."

"Whatever. So, who are we going to invite to the cookout?"

I took a moment to respond, as if I were mulling over that idea. I already knew that I wanted to invite Amanda's dad, but I was going to have to approach it gingerly.

"Maybe we could invite some people from work."

"Like who?"

"I think you should decide that."

"I barely know anybody at work."

"No problem. We have a few days for you to figure it out."

As we pulled into the firm's parking lot, I could feel Amanda's eyes on me.

"Whatever!" she muttered.

Amanda and I parted ways at the elevator. She's working on the 1st floor today, and my office is on the 5th floor.

"Are we meeting for lunch?"

"Not today. I have a meeting. See if you can find someone to join you. If not, there's a coffee shop around the corner. How about we meet at my office at 5 p.m.?"

"Gotcha," Amanda replied as I pushed the elevator button for the 5th floor.

Marge greeted me as I entered the office suite. "Where's Amanda?"

"I'm giving her wings."

"What's that mean?"

"She's on her own. She'll meet me here at the end of the day. And don't worry. She'll be fine."

Chapter 13

On the way home from work, Amanda enthusiastically told me about her day. She had done a lot of filing and copying, but her favorite job was collating some of the manuscripts that had arrived. She liked the two gals she was working with, and had gone to lunch with them.

"I think we should invite Judy and Patty to the cookout," she said. "Judy's single, but Patty's married and has a little boy. Is that OK?"

"Sure. You can invite them tomorrow. Anyone else?"

"We should definitely invite Myra. I'm working on the 2nd floor tomorrow, so I might meet some other people. What day and time are we having the cookout?"

"I was thinking Saturday. What do you think?"

"Yeah, Saturday's good. How about 2 p.m.?"

"That works for me."

We stopped at the grocery store to pick up something for dinner and buy some munchies. I got a rotisserie chicken and salad fixings, while Amanda found some snacks she liked. As we stood in the checkout lane, Amanda asked what the menu would be for our cookout.

"You can decide what we're having. We'll buy what we need after work on Friday."

From the store to my driveway, Amanda threw out ideas for the cookout menu. We agreed on grilled chicken, hamburgers, potato salad, and a tossed salad.

"I make some killer deviled eggs," I noted.

"Gross! But if you want them, you can make them. I'll make the potato salad."

Harvey made a big fuss over Amanda as we walked through the door. Amanda rubbed his back, and threw a toy for him to fetch.

"I'll put dinner together if you want to take Harvey out," I began to say, but they were already on their way to the yard. From the kitchen window I could hear Amanda telling Harvey all about her day.

As we finished eating, my cell phone rang. It was Betty. I excused myself and went out to the porch.

"What a nice surprise," I said when I took the call.

"I hope I'm not interrupting dinner."

"Not at all. We just finished, so Amanda gets to do the clean-up."

"How's it going?"

"Not bad," I replied, and began to tell Betty about the last few days. I was careful to stay positive in case Amanda could hear me from the kitchen.

"You're not telling me all the gory details. Is Amanda in the vicinity?"

"You've got that right,"

"So, are you having second thoughts?"

"Not at all!"

Changing the subject, I asked Betty what she'd been doing with her time since getting back from the monastery. She chatted about her busy days at work, and the humdrum activities of living alone like paying bills, doing the laundry, and taking out the trash.

"I'm jealous. You now have someone to help around the house," Betty remarked.

"Yeah. Right," I said somewhat facetiously. I told Betty about the cookout on Saturday, and invited her to join us.

"Gosh, I wish I could. Since it's a holiday weekend, I promised to volunteer at the local shelter. We're doing a barbecue for the homeless on Saturday."

"Wow, that's cool. I never think of doing things like that."

"It's in my blood. But I hope your cookout's a success."

I told Betty that Amanda was in charge of it, and that she was inviting some of the folks she worked with at her new job.

"Clever, Miss Victoria," Betty chuckled. "Very clever. I think you might be getting the hang of sharing your space."

"Well, maybe not totally yet, but I'll get it eventually."

By the time we said our goodbyes, dusk had descended, and Amanda was watching TV with Harvey. I went to turn out the kitchen light, and noticed that Amanda had put the leftovers in the refrigerator, but left the dishes in the sink. I rinsed them and put them in the dishwasher before joining my two free-loaders on the sofa.

"That was Betty," I said as I sat down.

"Uh huh." Amanda seemed deeply engrossed in her show.

"She said to tell you 'hi.'"

"Hi back to her."

I was quickly learning that TV was not something to be interrupted. I went to get my book in my bedroom, turning off the lights in the bathroom and Amanda's bedroom. By the time I returned to snuggle on the recliner, Amanda and Harvey were both snoozing.

^^^

After work the next day, I planned to set some ground rules with Amanda. I wasn't sure how to approach them, nor did I understand why I was reluctant to bring up the topic. I'm usually pretty direct in my expectations. Still, Amanda and I were just beginning to adjust to each other. I didn't want a confrontation; rather, I preferred to have a discussion about what we could both do to ensure a peaceful coexistence.

On the drive home, Amanda told me that she had invited Judy and Patty to the cookout. "Judy said yes right away, and Patty said she'd talk to her husband this evening. I told her she could bring her husband and kid. Is that OK?"

"Sure, that's fine. Did you decide on anyone else?"

"Yeah, I invited Linda, Peter, and Theresa from the 2ⁿᵈ floor." I recognized their names from some of the young new hires we had made during the past year.

"Good choices," I said.

"I think that's enough," Amanda noted.

"How about your dad?"

"What about him?"

"Do you want to invite your dad?"

"No! Absolutely not!"

"I'd like to invite him," I said. We rode the rest of the way in silence.

I made a quick stir-fry of leftover chicken and veggies for dinner while Amanda took Harvey out to the yard. I set the table, put kibbles in the bowl for Harvey, and called them in to eat. Over dessert, I decided to broach the intricacies of living together.

"I'd like to talk to you about some of the things you could do to help around the house."

"I've been helping."

"Yes, you have, but I think we need a little more even distribution."

"Like what?"

"How about we make a deal that whoever does the cooking, doesn't have to clean up?"

"I cleaned up yesterday when you got a phone call."

"Yes, you did, and I appreciated it. But more was needed. Cleaned up means you put the leftovers in containers in the refrigerator, you rinse and put the dishes in the dishwasher, and you wipe off the table. When everything's done, you turn out the light." Amanda rolled her eyes. "So, tonight, since I made dinner, would you be willing to clean up?"

"No problem. I'll cook tomorrow and you can clean up. What else?"

"Speaking of lights," I said, "electricity is expensive. When you leave a room, you turn out the lights."

"Geez! You sound like my dad."

"Unless you're willing to pay the electric bill, do we have a deal?"

"Whatever."

"When you bring a beverage to the living room or your bedroom, you bring the glass back to the kitchen and put it in the dishwasher. And, if you have a snack at night, ask me if I'd like one, too. I'll do the same for you."

"Gotcha," Amanda said with a little sarcasm. "Anything else?"

"Yes. I'd like you to invite your dad to the cookout."

With that, Amanda stormed out of the kitchen, and slammed the door to her bedroom.

^^^

I decided to get some fresh air. Harvey followed me across the yard, his tail wagging when he saw Myra sitting on her porch.

"How's everything going?" Myra asked as she motioned for me to have a seat.

"OK, I guess. Well, maybe less than OK right now."

"What happened?"

"I tried to set some ground rules, but Amanda got herself in a knot and locked herself in her room." Myra burst out laughing.

"It's not funny. I wanted it to be a discussion, not a confrontation. I think I messed up."

When I told Myra what had transpired, and what I had said to get Amanda so upset, she just chuckled.

"You didn't use psychology. You can't rely on business skills when dealing with a kid who's used to doing things her way. You have to use psychology."

"All right. Teach me some psychology."

"It sounds to me like you started off OK when you discussed sharing some of the household tasks, but then you got into the boss role of 'do this' and 'don't do that.' On top of it all, you told her that she could pick the guests at the cookout, and then you made the decision to invite her father. It sounds like she doesn't want him there."

"I want her to mend fences with him."

"That's what you want, but that's obviously not what she's ready for. Give her some slack on that one, but keep her motivated to help out around the house. I told you this wasn't going to be easy."

"You're right about that! By the way, Amanda did want you to come to the cookout."

"Then, let her invite me."

I wondered if I really would ever do and say the right things when it came to Amanda.

"You come over any time you want to vent. I've got a bunch of tricks up my sleeve."

"I have no doubt of that," I laughed and made my way across the grass, Harvey trailing behind me.

Once inside, I noticed that Amanda was still in her room, and the dishes were still on the table. I put the bits of leftovers in the garbage, giving the last few nibbles of chicken to Harvey. Then I locked the doors, turned out the lights, and went to bed.

Chapter 14

When I arrived at the kitchen for breakfast the next morning, I noticed that everything from the night before had been cleaned up, and Amanda had set the table for breakfast. She had even fed Harvey his kibbles and had let him out to do his duty. Seeing my surprise, Amanda said, "I'm sorry."

"Apology accepted. And I'm sorry for insisting that your dad be invited to your cookout. I was out of line."

"Give me time."

"I will," I promised.

After work, we decided to pick up sandwiches at the deli. "It doesn't feel right," I remarked, "that I'll have an easy clean up night."

"It seems right to me. I don't have to make supper. Besides, we have to make our shopping list for the cookout."

"Did you invite Myra?"

"Not yet. I'll go over after we eat."

We chatted comfortably about Amanda's fourth day at work and how much she enjoyed what she was doing. She really liked the people she worked with, and she said that she could see why I had stayed with the firm so long.

"You make me sound like a dinosaur."

"Well, 39 years is a really long time. Are you going to retire soon?"

"I don't know. It's a big decision, and I'm not sure what to do."

"Well, I think you should stay. Everyone I talk to thinks you're awesome."

"Well, thank you, Amanda. You'll be the first person I tell when I make up my mind."

I cleaned up while Amanda took Harvey for a walk. On her way home, she stopped to invite Myra to the barbecue.

"Myra's coming to the cookout," Amanda announced when she returned, "and she's bringing a pie."

"That's great! Myra's famous for her pies."

"She's a cool lady. I can see why you like her."

I had a feeling that Myra had pulled a trick or two out of her sleeve.

As we finished writing our shopping list, Amanda said, "I'm going to get some milk and cookies. Do you want some?"

"I think I'll make a cup of tea to go with those cookies you picked out at the store," I replied with a smile.

^^^

Amanda's cookout was a tremendous success. She made the salads the night before, while I made the deviled eggs and marinated the chicken. On Saturday morning, Amanda got the lawn chairs out of the garage, and set up the folding table in the yard. I prepped the hamburgers, and arranged the sodas in a cooler filled with ice.

Amanda wanted to start cooking the chicken early to make sure it was done by the time her guests began to arrive. I told her I'd do the hamburgers on the grill, if she'd do the entertaining. As cars were pulling into the driveway, I was happy to see Myra traipse across the yard with her pie, and she gallantly made herself a part of the festivities.

After our meal, some of the young folks were playing a game of badminton in the yard; others were playing whiffle ball.

"I wonder where she found that equipment," I mused to Myra.

"I'm guilty. I told Amanda the other night that she could look through my garage to see if she could find any games to play. Grandmas need to be prepared with the right tools."

"You're mighty clever. I can see I have a lot of learning to do."

"How are you doing with the psychology?"

"I think it's working. Amanda and I are going to watch the fireworks on TV tonight. Why don't you join us?"

"That's past my bedtime. I'm going to help you put away the leftovers, then I'm going home."

As we were covering the salads and putting them in the refrigerator, Amanda popped into the kitchen.

"Everyone's going to town to watch the fireworks," she said excitedly. "Patty said I can ride with her. Do you mind if I go?"

It took everything I had not to gasp. I composed myself and said, "Not at all. You go and have a great time."

"Awesome!" Amanda replied as ran out the door.

"You look perplexed," Myra noted when we were alone.

"I am. When we discussed the town fireworks the other day, Amanda said they were dorky and an 'expression of the establishment.' I actually thought she was afraid of them, which is why I suggested that we stay home and watch the TV special."

"Well, you handled it well," Myra chuckled.

We glanced out the window and saw Amanda directing everyone to help with the cleanup. The guys were lugging the table and chairs to the garage; the gals had a large trash bag and were collecting all of the used paper plates and plastic cutlery. Harvey was making sure he found any tidbits left on the ground.

I heard Amanda say, "We've got to make sure there's no mess left. Victoria likes order."

Myra and I were both laughing and she said, "On that note, I'm going to say goodnight. I don't think you have anything to worry about with that girl. I can see what you saw in her."

"I'm so glad you came today, Myra." I walked her to the door.

Amanda called out that they were on their way, and that she'd be home right after the fireworks. I waved goodbye as the young folks loaded into their cars.

Amanda came through the front door just as the 11 p.m. news was starting. Harvey bounded over to her with his tail wagging.

"You didn't have to wait up for me," she said.

"I didn't. I was just going to watch the news. Come tell me about the fireworks." Amanda and Harvey joined me on the sofa.

"I had a good time. The best part was watching the kids. They were waving their little flags, and their eyes got big every time the sky lit up with the sparkling lights. It was cool."

"I thought maybe everyone would be going out after the fireworks."

"Some of them were going to a club for drinks, but the ones with families were going home. I was kind of tired. Besides, I'm underage and would have been carded," Amanda noted with a mischievous grin.

"Good decision. I enjoyed your cookout today."

"I did, too. Everybody said it was fun. Is there any leftover pie?"

"There's one piece left with your name on it."

"Cool! Come on, Harvey-boy. Let's see what's in the refrigerator."

Chapter 15

Through the next week, Amanda and I had gotten into a fairly comfortable routine. Occasionally we'd get on each other's nerves, but we had learned ways to give each other some space. Harvey liked the fact that Amanda would take him on a long walk when she wanted time to herself.

On the following Saturday, we planned a trip to the mall after lunch. I wanted to go to the department store, but Amanda preferred the trendier specialty shops. We agreed to meet at 3:30 p.m. for a beverage at the food court.

Apparently, I was the first to arrive, so I sat at a table near the entrance. I was deep in thought when I heard, "What do you think, Victoria?"

I almost fell off my chair! There in front of me stood Amanda with an attractive new hairstyle. The neon highlights were gone.

"Oh, my gosh, Amanda. What did you do?"

She laughed and said, "Don't you love it?" as she turned and modeled. "I was so lucky they had a cancelation just as I walked in to get an appointment. I wanted to surprise you."

"Wow! You look gorgeous!"

We went to a kiosk and made our beverage choices, then peeked into each other's bags when we returned to our table. Amanda had gotten an attractive new top that she could wear at the office, and I had purchased a pair of casual pants from the clearance rack. Amanda scrunched up her nose.

"What are you going to wear with those?"

"I don't know. I'll find something."

"They're ugly, and they have an elastic waist."

"That's what happens when you get old."

"That's a bunch of crap. They're going to make you look old."

"I'm just going to wear them around the house."

"It doesn't matter. Besides, you need to update your wardrobe for work. I'll help you pick out some tops that'll be utterly awesome."

When we returned to the department store, Amanda selected two different designs, and insisted I try them on. Neither was my style but, despite my protests, she pushed me into the dressing room. I tried on the first one that had lots of color, but the neckline was slightly lower than I usually wear. I pulled back the curtain and Amanda whistled.

"That looks great on you. The swirls of blue really bring out your blue eyes. We'll take it."

The other was made of some type of stretchy fabric that seemed to hug all the right parts. It, too, had a colorful pattern, beyond what I'd typically wear. When I stepped out of the dressing room, Amanda declared it was another winner.

Still hesitant, I paid for my wares. Amanda seemed really pleased with herself. She led me over to the jewelry counter, and she picked out a colorful necklace for each of us, matching the colors in our new purchases.

"This is my gift to you. I really appreciate all you've done for me."

"You don't have to do that, but thank you. It's lovely. Since it's already supper time, why don't we get something to eat? There's a family restaurant up the road, close to the multiplex theater. Are you too tired to go to the movies?"

"Are you kidding? The night has just begun!"

We both laughed. I was thinking that I must be crazy.

We checked out the movies playing and, though I thought better of it, I let Amanda choose. To my surprise, she picked out one we'd both enjoy, and she even volunteered to pick up our tickets before we ate so we wouldn't have to stand in line later. We had enough time for a casual meal before returning to the theater.

On the way home, we chuckled about the characters in the romantic comedy, and I could tell that Amanda had enjoyed the day. I had to admit that I did, too.

^^^

As we got ready for work on Monday, Amanda insisted that I wear one of my new tops and necklace with a pantsuit she chose from my closet. As we walked into the firm, I was aware of the furtive glances coming my way. Amanda beamed as she said good morning, by name, to each person we met along the way.

When we got to the elevator, she whispered, "They think you look really nice." I rolled my eyes.

"Well, don't you look pretty today," Marge said as I stepped into my office.

"Amanda's working on me," I laughed.

"She's doing a great job. Those colors make you look ten years younger!" I blushed as I tried to make myself look busy.

"You know, that girl's really something. The folks downstairs have remarked about how accomplished she is. Not only is her work done well, but she takes the time to give a personal greeting to each person she meets. They're going to be sad to see her leave at the end of the summer." I was starting to think the same thing myself.

On the way home, I asked Amanda if she wanted to drive.

"I don't have my license yet."

I could tell it was a sore subject, but I pressed on. Because her father didn't like the crowd she had hung around with, he had refused to let her get a learner's permit, Amanda noted. I suggested that she call him after supper and broach the subject again.

"If he approves, I'll teach you how to drive."

Later that evening, I heard Amanda telling her father about work, and how much she was enjoying her stay. Toward the end of the conversation, she inquired if she could get her learner's permit. He must have asked to speak with me because she handed me the phone and made a face.

I assured Mr. Angeli that I had brought up the topic, and I felt that Amanda had demonstrated that she was a responsible young woman. He gave his approval, and agreed to mail a permission letter in the morning.

I nodded a yes to Amanda, and handed back the phone. She squealed and screeched her excited thank you's. We would get the paperwork and manual after work the next day.

Chapter 16

Two nights later, we decided to cook out on the grill again, and I called Myra to see if she wanted to join us for dinner. "I can always throw another potato on the grill," I cajoled.

"It doesn't take much to convince me. I was planning on heating up leftovers. How about I bring a pie I baked yesterday?"

When Myra arrived, Amanda was setting the table.

"Well, don't you look pretty," Myra said. "I love your new hair-do. It's very becoming."

Amanda thanked her, and told her about our plans for driving lessons.

Myra laughed and said, "I remember those days. I'm glad I don't have to do that anymore. Speaking of driving, my granddaughter, Kate, is coming to visit this weekend. She's about your age, Amanda, and I thought you might enjoy getting together."

"That'd be cool. I'd like to meet her."

When Kate arrived on Friday after work, the four of us went out to dinner. Kate's blond hair was pulled up in an attractive ponytail that seemed to match her playful personality. We were seated at a booth, Myra and Kate on one side, Amanda and I on the other, so that the girls sat across from each other.

Myra explained that Kate's family had relocated about an hour away after her dad's company built a new office complex a few years ago.

"That was a tough move," Kate said. "I was just starting high school, and didn't want to leave my friends."

"I didn't like it either," Myra said. "Your grandfather was sick, and I knew it would be hard to care for him without your mom and dad's help." I remembered what a challenging time that had been for Myra.

"I know. When grandpop died, dad wanted you to move in with us."

"I definitely considered the offer, but my memories are here. And I'm not ready to give up my independence!"

The waiter took our orders and we settled into casual talk, munching on delectable warm bread while we waited for our plates to arrive. Somehow we got on the topic of Kate's going to culinary school in the fall. Amanda asked all kinds of questions and, before you knew it, the girls were deep in conversation.

Myra winked at me with a mischievous grin. By the time we paid our check, Amanda and Kate had decided to spend Saturday baking at Myra's house, with a contest to see who made the best dessert. Myra and I were to be the judges.

∧∧∧

With Saturday morning to myself, I threw in a load of laundry, brewed a cup of tea, and called Betty.

"What a surprise!" she exclaimed when she heard my voice. "I was just thinking of you!"

"We must have mental telepathy."

"So, how's it going with Amanda?"

I proceeded to tell Betty about Amanda's job at my firm, and that she was doing well. Already she was making friends, and her cookout had been a success.

"So, what aren't you telling me?"

"Do you mean like the times she's given me the silent treatment, or locked herself in her room?"

Betty laughed out loud. I proceeded to tell Betty about the house rules fiasco, and the advice that Myra had given me about using psychology.

"Myra sounds like a smart lady."

I agreed, and told Betty that Myra's granddaughter was visiting, and that the girls seemed to have similar interests.

"They're both the same age, and they both like to cook. In fact, they're having a dessert throw-down next door, as we speak. Myra and I will be the judges."

"I wondered why you were able to speak so freely. It sounds like you're doing fine."

"I think we are. The funny thing is, I think I'm helping Amanda develop career skills, and she's working on a makeover for me."

"Does she think she can teach an old dog new tricks?"

I told Betty about our shopping trip, and the outfits she picked out for me. "They're definitely not my style, but she's having fun with it. And I'm learning when to back off and let her be herself."

Betty caught me up on what she had been doing and said she had been in touch with Maggie.

"She and Ted are doing better. They've started to go to counseling and are working on their communication. I think it's a good sign."

I agreed, and told Betty about seeing them paddling the canoe on the lake my last day at the monastery.

Speaking of monastery," Betty interrupted, "I'm going back for the last week of August. Why don't you see if there's another cabin available at the same time?"

"Hmmm. That's not a bad idea. I had planned to take another week off this summer, and it would be around the time that Amanda will be going home. I could drop her off on my way there."

"Sounds like a plan!"

When I disconnected, I called Sr. Tony. I was in luck. I booked the last available poustinia. Tony asked me how Amanda was doing, and I told her much of what I had told Betty. Of course, I left out the gory details.

Later that afternoon, Myra and I declared a tie in the dessert throw-down. Kate made a delicious berry pie using her grandmother's recipe, and Amanda outdid herself with attractively decorated chocolate cupcakes. They had done a good job cleaning up the kitchen, and we encouraged them to go see a movie and enjoy the evening.

^^^

The girls had conspired to prepare an early dinner at my house on Sunday, with Myra and me as invited guests. They planned their menu, shopped for ingredients, and declared the kitchen off-limits. I busied myself with paying bills and catching up on some paperwork. Harvey planted himself under their feet so he wouldn't miss any morsels they dropped from the counter.

Amanda's touch was evident in the table setting. She had located a white tablecloth and my good dinnerware from the china closet. In the center of the table, she had placed a floral arrangement that she made from daisies she found in the yard, and added two lit candles on either side of it.

The first course was an attractive mix of arugula and baby green spinach with a light vinaigrette and homemade croutons. The main course consisted of crusted sautéed chicken breasts with a delectable creamy mushroom gravy, garlic roasted green beans, and mashed potatoes. A warm apple crisp with a dollop of whipped cream was served for dessert.

"You two have outdone yourselves!" Myra exclaimed.

I added that they could start a restaurant. Their food was delicious, and it was attractively plated.

Kate admitted that it was her goal to be a chef, but that Amanda's design talent was far better than hers.

"I've decided that I'd like to go to culinary school," Amanda said.

"That's a great idea, Amanda," I replied, and everyone concurred.

"Amada and I talked about it today, and I gave her the school's web address so she can check it out," Kate said. "Wouldn't it be cool if you can start with me in the fall?"

Without trying to dampen their enthusiasm, I pointed out that there's an admission and financial aid process that might take longer than a month. We all agreed that Amanda should explore her options.

The girls sent Myra and me to the front porch while they cleaned up, despite our protests of wanting to help. When we were alone, I thanked Myra for inviting her granddaughter to visit.

"I'm glad they got along so well. It really is amazing how much they complement each other."

"Kate ignited a passion in Amanda that I don't believe she thought was possible. I was worried about what would happen when Amanda got back into the environment of her old crowd, but culinary school might set her on course for success."

On that note, the girls joined us, and Kate said she had to be on her way. Amanda went with Kate to gather her things, and Myra followed. I picked up the phone to call Amanda's dad to give him a quick "head's up" about the culinary school idea.

Chapter 17

The next few weeks whizzed by. Amanda got her learner's permit, and I began teaching her how to drive each evening after work. With her dad's support, she also applied to the same culinary school that Kate planned to attend.

Toward the end of July, on a particularly hectic day of interviews and business meetings, Marge popped into my office and asked who the young man was that Amanda had been seeing at lunch the past few days. Apparently, a few of the other employees had been concerned about the arrogant character who had caused a ruckus when security wouldn't give him access to the building.

"I have no idea. Amanda hasn't mentioned that she met anyone, least of all anyone who might be a concern. Why wasn't I aware of the security issue?"

"Have you been reading your e-mails?"

"I have to admit, these days have been so busy that I've only scrolled through for the ones that looked important."

"I guess I should have mentioned it to you, but I didn't think too much of it until Judy and Patty from the editorial department shared their concerns with me. They said that Amanda's been meeting this guy at the coffee shop around the corner. Yesterday, Amanda invited the gals to join her and the 'condescending jerk' for lunch, that's what Patty called him, but he got angry and stormed out. Judy said that Amanda ran after him, and they seemed to be having an argument on the street."

"I can't tell you how much I appreciate that you told me about this," I stated, visibly distressed.

"I didn't mean to upset you, nor did I want to rat on Amanda. We all love her, and don't want to see her get hurt. I don't really know any other details. Unfortunately, I need to remind you that your executive committee meeting is scheduled to start in just a few minutes."

As I gathered my portfolio and headed toward the elevator, I was seething with anger. I had no doubt in my mind that Amanda had somehow reconnected with Derek. I could barely concentrate throughout the meeting as I dealt with my emotions. I gave a cursory weekly report, and was scarcely able to process my colleagues' commentaries.

How could Amanda do this? How could she betray my trust and sneak behind my back to meet up with the very person that her father tried to keep at bay?

I was jolted back to reality when I realized that the meeting was over, and everyone was departing the conference room.

"Are you OK, Victoria?" asked one of my associates. "You don't seem like yourself today."

I tried to shake my distress, and replied that I must be a little tired from the busy week we had.

He laughed and said, "It was a doozie! Do something fun with Amanda this weekend. You both deserve it!"

Yeah, right, I thought to myself as I returned to my office. How in the world was I going to handle this one? I glanced at my watch and noticed that it was close to 6 p.m. Marge would have already departed for the day, and Amanda was probably waiting for me. I wouldn't have time to give a frantic call to Betty, asking her advice on how to deal with the situation.

Amanda greeted me with a disgruntled hello as I opened my office door.

"Don't you know when the day is done? Come on, it's Friday. Let's bust this place!" she said in a grumpy tone.

I bit my tongue, knowing that if I responded it would unleash my emotions. I methodically straightened my desk, and gathered a few papers I wanted to take home. After retrieving my purse from the file cabinet, I announced that I was ready.

I kept my counsel in the car, though Amanda chatted incessantly about inconsequential trivia.

"Do you want to go to the movies tonight?" Amanda queried.

"Not really."

I guess she realized that I was miffed because she said, "OK, I'm sorry I was impatient when you got out late from your meeting. I know it wasn't your fault."

"Right."

"So, let's do something fun. You want to go to the mall?"

I thought about my options. If I exploded before I had time to think about my approach in discussing Amanda's clandestine meetings with Derek, there would be no resolution. We'd have a major battle. Just dropping Amanda off at the mall could lead to her finding a way to call Derek and asking him to meet her there.

"Yes, we can go to the mall."

"Cool! Today's pay day, and I've had my eye on this really neat outfit I could get for work."

"How about if you do your shopping, and we meet at the food court in about an hour?"

Amanda thought that was a great idea. Once I was alone, I found an out of the way table at the food court, and searched for Betty's number in my phone contacts. Thank goodness she picked up after the second ring.

"I was just thinking about calling you tonight," Betty chuckled. "We must have radar!"

"I need your words of wisdom."

"Uh oh. What's going on?"

I recounted what Marge had told me, and relayed my suspicions that Amanda was meeting up with Derek.

"But you don't know that for sure. So before you get yourself in a frenzy, don't you think you need to ask Amanda about the guy she was meeting?"

"I'm already agitated. In fact, I'm so angry with Amanda that I don't even know how to approach the topic with her."

"Why are you angry?"

"Why am I angry? You want to know why I'm angry?"

It was obvious that my voice had increased by several decibels.

"I can hear that you're upset. But I want you to express what's triggering your emotions."

"I'm not really sure. I think I feel betrayed."

"OK. Let's say it really was Derek that Amanda has been seeing. Do you feel betrayed that she'd want to meet with him?"

"If Amanda had told me that she wanted to bring closure to her past relationship with Derek, I probably could have supported her. She didn't have to sneak around behind my back."

"So, it's more of a betrayal because you didn't know about her alleged meetings. What else do you feel?"

"I guess I feel that I let Amanda's dad down. He trusted her to my care. He wanted her away from those former so-called friends, and I couldn't protect her."

"If Amanda did get together with Derek, were you an accomplice?"

"No, of course not."

"Is it possible, then, that your expression of inadequacy is unfounded? Amanda's father wasn't able to guard her from acquaintances, so who are you to think you could do a better job? Amanda's a young adult. She may need guidance, but certainly not shielding."

Betty made a lot of sense, and I could feel my emotions settling. We spent the better part of an hour rationally discussing options for how I might handle a conversation with Amanda without a volatile escalation. We chit-chatted a while longer, until I saw Amanda searching the food court for me. As Betty and I said our farewells, I waved Amanda over to my table.

After Amanda and I selected our dinner options and finished eating, she pulled out a small gift-wrapped box and encouraged me to open it.

"What's this?"

"It's for you. Open it."

Inside was an attractive decorative pin of a giraffe.

"You need something on the lapel of that suit you're wearing. I picked the giraffe because it reminded me of how you're helping me reach high above what I ever thought I could achieve."

I was speechless. "Thank you, Amanda," I said simply. "I will treasure it."

"Now, I need your advice." Amanda said. "Something happened at work that I don't know how to handle."

Amanda proceeded to tell me that one of the staff had taken a picture of her in front of the firm, and had posted it on Facebook, tagging her as "Employee of the Month." Some of her former friends saw the photo and contacted Derek. He came looking for her.

"He caused a big stir in the lobby when he wasn't allowed in," Amanda explained.

"I heard there was a security problem the other day."

"Yeah, well, I was delivering mail when I saw him. I took him to the coffee shop so we could talk, and I explained that I wasn't interested in hooking up again. He got really mad, like it was my fault that we broke up. Can you believe it? So, anyway, Derek sent me an e-mail at work—I don't know how he got my e-mail address—and asked me to meet him for lunch the next day. I didn't want to be alone with him so when I saw Judy and Patty come in, I asked them to join us. Derek went bonkers. We argued outside, and I told him that if he ever bothered me again, I'd call the cops."

"Why didn't you tell me all of this, Amanda?"

"I didn't want you to be angry with me for meeting with Derek. I thought I could handle it, but I made a mess. Now I don't know what to do. Derek's got a temper, and if he's on drugs, he can be really mean."

"The first thing we've got to do is to notify our firm's security department and they can deal with informing the police. I'll call them tonight. We'll also contact tech services and have them change your e-mail address. Did you tell him that you're staying with me?"

"No, I wouldn't do that. Please don't tell my dad."

"I can't promise that, Amanda. Let's let Security handle an inquiry, and they can make the decision about who needs to be informed. In the meantime, you and I have had quite a day. How about we go home and snuggle up with Harvey?"

"I'm really sorry," Amanda said on the drive back to my house. I glanced at her forlorn face.

"You have nothing to be sorry for. You did the right thing by leading Derek to a less controversial setting, and by making it clear that he was unwelcome at the firm and in your life. If he's stupid enough to contact you again, the authorities will take a stand. And you know what else?"

"What?"

"I'm really proud of you!"

^^^

I called Betty the next morning while Amanda was taking Harvey for a walk. I was hoping she wasn't busy, and relieved when she answered the phone.

"You'll never believe what happened last evening after I spoke to you."

"You met an eligible bachelor at the mall?"

"No, I'm serious." I told her of Amanda's request for help. "Thank goodness I talked to you first, and had dealt with my temper. I was ready to confront Amanda, though I knew it would end badly. Instead, I learned that Derek has been stalking her, and she was trying to keep him away from the firm." I filled Betty in on the details.

"So, how are you feeling now?"

"I'm relieved that Amanda confided in me and explained the situation. I'm also kicking myself for jumping to conclusions before I knew the facts."

I told Betty that I had contacted the security director when we got home, and he notified the police. I also noted that I had called our tech support department, and they assured me that Amanda's e-mail address would be changed immediately. They'll monitor her incoming mail.

"It sounds like you've covered all of the bases, alerting the proper authorities," Betty said. "I also agree that you overacted when you thought that Amanda was secretly meeting with Derek. Don't you think it's time that you just relax and enjoy this experience of sharing your home with another person? You don't always have to be the corporate executive."

Betty's comment annoyed me, particularly because I didn't see myself in that light.

"Actually, Miss Smarty Pants, Amanda and I have a comfortable relationship. Even last night, she bought me a gift to express her appreciation of how much I've helped her."

"Uh huh. Do you hear yourself? How much you've helped her, like you're the boss and she should honor and respect you? Give me a break, oh mighty one. How about a nod to Amanda for conveying her friendship in a tangible way. What have you given to Amanda? And don't give me some crass line about providing her a job and a place to live. She has a home and a dad who loves her."

"Whoa! I thought you supported my invitation to Amanda that she stay with me this summer."

"I definitely agreed that it was a good idea, given the situation. And I'm not belittling you for all that you've done for Amanda. Despite your age differences, think of her as a new friend. She has as much to offer you as you have to share with her. Don't be afraid to let her see you as a woman who can laugh as readily as you can cry, one who admits her weaknesses and uses her strengths to help others. You're an authentic woman, Victoria, but you've spent many years building an aura of competence."

"I am competent!"

"Of course you are. If you weren't, you'd never have risen to your level of leadership. Let me put it this way. When we met at the monastery, you and I were on equal playing fields. We're both about the same age, we're both professionals, and we have many of the same interests. We became friends right away, because we didn't have to prove anything to each other. We could be ourselves, and even share our inner feelings."

"Yeah, but Amanda's not my age. It's different."

"You're not her mother, nor are you her guardian," Betty said. "Remember the expression that people come into our lives for a reason. Amanda and I are now a part of your life. Think of the purpose of that in terms of what it means for you, rather than what you're doing for us."

"Those are powerful words. I think I need to mull about what you've said."

"Well, don't take them too seriously," Betty said with a chuckle. "Remember, I'm a lawyer. We like to argue. And on that note, I'm going to let you go. I'm meeting Maggie for lunch, and I don't want to be late."

I poured myself a cup of tea, then sat at the kitchen table to ponder our conversation. As usual, Betty's wisdom gave me another perspective to think about.

When Amanda and Harvey returned from their walk I said, "Hey, Amanda. How about we go to the movies this afternoon?"

Chapter 18

Amanda got her letter of acceptance to culinary school during the first week of August. She was more excited than I had ever seen her. She handed me the letter, and ran to get the phone to call Kate and her dad. I could hear Kate's squeals of joy from the next room. They made plans to get together on the weekend so they could coordinate their preparations.

Amanda's dad also seemed pleased that Amanda was so happy. After he and Amanda chatted for a few minutes, she handed me the receiver and said he wanted to talk to me.

"Hi, Steve. Amanda received good news, don't you think?"

"It's great news! I never thought that Amanda might be interested in a culinary career. I knew that she inherited her mother's flair for design, but she didn't seem to be focused on art. She did take a cooking class once, and she said she enjoyed it, but I don't ever remember seeing this much passion. Heck, I don't think she ever cooked a full meal around here."

"I was a little surprised myself. I think the idea formed when she met my neighbor's granddaughter, Kate."

I told him about their cooking contests and how well they get along together. "When you meet Kate, you'll see why they've become good friends."

"What do I need to do?" Steve asked. "I'm kind of at a loss. My wife always knew the right thing to do or say, especially with Amanda. And I think Amanda's still miffed that I sent her to that monastery."

"Just be supportive. She loves you very much, and she wants your affirmation. Probably more than you know."

Amanda's enthusiasm about culinary school intensified when her dad said she could share a studio apartment with Kate in the fall. Once the excitement died down, I reminded Amanda that the acceptance letter included a form for a physical and some immunizations. She also needed a TB test. I told her that I'd set up an appointment with my physician, and hoped she could fit Amanda in without much delay.

Amanda's last week was a whirlwind of activity. Between driving practice, shopping, and packing, Amanda had been invited to lunch each day. The general office staff had a farewell party for her on Thursday, and her doctor appointment was Friday. We planned to leave on Saturday.

"I wish you hadn't made arrangements to go to the cabin next week," Amanda said one evening as she was in the driver's seat.

"Come to a complete stop at the corner," I cautioned. She rolled her eyes.

"I think it's perfect timing," I said. "School starts just after Labor Day, and you need to spend some time getting ready for your new adventure. Your dad's going to go with you to get your driver's license, and I'm going to try to get used to you not being around." I looked at her and added, "I'm going to miss you. Seriously."

"Me, too." I think we were both a little misty eyed.

^^^

We arrived a few minutes early for the doctor's appointment on Friday afternoon. Amanda said her final farewells at the firm in the morning, and I took the afternoon off. I picked up a magazine while Amanda was called to the examining room. She assured me that she had brought the necessary forms, and my presence wasn't needed.

Forty minutes later, one of the nurses asked me to follow her to the examining room. I told myself it was probably just some formality, but butterflies invaded my stomach. The nurse opened the door, and I could see that my doctor was sitting on her stool next to Amanda, who was perched on the end of the examining table. Dr. White had her hand on Amanda's knee. Amanda looked as pale as a ghost as I entered the room, and it was evident that she had been crying. My nervousness turned to fear as I gazed at each of them.

Amanda looked at me, and said in a shaky voice, "I'm pregnant."

I enveloped Amanda with my arms and stroked her hair as she sobbed. Dr. White explained that she had noticed some physical evidence during her examination, and ran a pregnancy test. It was positive.

"I calculate that Amanda's about four months pregnant, with the baby due in January."

Dr. White pulled out a desk chair and invited me to sit. As Amanda calmed down, I asked if she suspected that she was pregnant. She shook her head no. She murmured that her period had always been irregular, and Derek assured her that women couldn't get pregnant the first time.

"That's not true," Dr. White told Amanda. "Not only can you get pregnant, but you can also get an STD. I think we'd better test for those, too."

I had a million questions for Amanda, and I wanted to punch the jerk who took advantage of an innocent girl who had no mother to lead her to womanhood.

Dr. White was very compassionate and very clear in her directives. "Although I'm going to write a prescription for vitamins, you need prenatal care, Amanda," she said. "I can recommend an excellent obstetrician who has a practice not too far from your home, and I want you to make an appointment as soon as you can. I'll send in the nurse to give you your immunizations for school. All of the required shots are safe during pregnancy." Amanda nodded that she understood.

Dr. White stood and said to me, "Amanda told me what you've done for her this summer, Victoria, and that she'll be going home tomorrow. I think she's going to need some assistance to tell her father."

I agreed, and asked if this would hinder her plans to start school.

"I don't believe it should," Dr. White said. "Amanda's healthy and, barring any unforeseen complications, she should have a routine pregnancy."

She turned to Amanda. "I know the news came as a shock to you today, Amanda, but this is a very special time for you and your baby. You have people who love you and will help you." Amanda was crying softly when Dr. White left the room.

The nurse returned with some samples of vitamins, her prescription, the signed health forms, and the immunizations. When she finished, we gathered our things and quietly left. The silence on our way home was deafening.

Neither of us felt much like going out to dinner as we had previously planned. I suggested that we just order a pizza.

"Whatever," Amanda said.

When we arrived at the house, Amanda went into her room and closed the door. I made a cup of tea and sat on the porch, mulling how quickly the twists and turns of life can occur.

I called for pizza delivery, then imagined how difficult the next day would be for Amanda. I contemplated cancelling my plans to go to the cabin, but realized that this was a time that Amanda was going to need to be with family. I thought about calling her dad to give him a heads-up, but decided against it. It's not the kind of news to get over the phone.

The pizza arrived, and I brought it to the kitchen counter after paying the delivery boy. The aroma wafted through the house, but Amanda didn't stir. I tapped lightly on her door and, getting no response, peeked in. She had cried herself to sleep, with Harvey snuggled up beside her.

Chapter 19

I n the morning, Amanda was still a little pale, emphasized by the dark circles under her eyes. I made her favorite pancakes and hoped they would cajole her to eat. We sat across from each other at the bistro table in the kitchen.

"Do you want to talk?" I asked gently.

Amanda nodded and said, "How could I have been so stupid, Victoria? My dad's going to kill me!"

"You weren't stupid, Amanda. You were gullible... and your father will not kill you. I promise. I agree he'll probably be upset at first, but his primary concern will be taking care of you."

Harvey sidled up to Amanda, rubbing against her leg. He could sense her emotions. Amanda reached down, aimlessly stroking his head.

"I thought being pregnant would be a happy time. I wanted a family and a home."

"I remember. And that can still happen, just not the way you dreamed."

"Did you tell my dad?"

"No, I think you need to do that in person. But I'll be with you to help. I've given it a lot of thought. I'm going to continue with my plans, and I think you should, too. Decisions can't be made until your mind is settled. You need to be able to rationally determine all of your options. In the meantime, next week you can see an obstetrician, and organize the things you need to take to school. Let your dad help you."

I began to clean up the kitchen, while Amanda skootched her last pancake around in the syrup.

"Do you think I should tell Kate?" Amanda asked.

"I think you should tell your father first. Once he has a chance to process the news then, yes, you should call Kate. Now, why don't you start to gather your things and pack the car. I'm going to bring Harvey over to Myra's."

Amanda looked up at me with those big brown eyes. "And, no, I'm not going to tell Myra until you tell me I may," I added.

By the time I had returned from dropping off Harvey, Amanda had her bags loaded and was beginning on mine. I collected the food that I had packed the night before, and added the refrigerated items at the last minute. Amanda stood in the doorway, gazing as if she were memorizing every detail. I walked over and gave her a big hug, tears stinging my eyes.

^^^

We arrived at Amanda's house shortly after noon. Her dad was in the kitchen making BLT's, and he had tied a big helium balloon to her chair with colorful ribbons. It said, "Congratulations!"

"Welcome home, honey," Steve Angeli said as he walked toward Amanda, wiping his hands on his pants. He gave her a big hug. He didn't seem to notice the bags under her eyes despite taking a long look at her.

"Wow! You look beautiful!"

Remembering that I was standing there, Steve turned to me and said, "Thank you so much, Victoria, for all you've done for Amanda."

"Look, honey. I got you a balloon to celebrate all of your accomplishments."

The irony wasn't lost on Amanda, but she smiled wanly and said, "Thanks, dad. I really like it."

"Have a seat," Amanda's dad said as he gestured to the kitchen table and began to plate the sandwiches. He opened a bag of chips, and got some pickles from the refrigerator.

"I can't tell you how good it is to see you, Amanda. I've really missed you."

"I've really missed you, too, dad."

I could tell that Amanda was very nervous. Her dad took a big mouthful of his sandwich, and I followed his lead. Might as well bite the bullet, I thought as I dabbed my mouth with a napkin. I cleared my throat.

"Mr. Angeli," I began tentatively, glancing at Amanda. "I'm afraid that Amanda had some unsettling news yesterday. We didn't call because I thought she should tell you in person."

Amanda's dad put his sandwich on the plate. Amanda's eyes filled with tears.

"Go on, Amanda," I said, looking intently at her. "You can do this."

"I don't think I can."

"Amanda, I've always said that you can tell me anything," Steve reassured her. "If you've changed your mind about school, or if..."

Amanda interrupted her father in mid-sentence. "I'm pregnant."

Steve exhaled with his lips pursed. It came out almost like a low gaspy whistle. He looked at me, and I nodded slowly.

He took several deep breaths and then said, "When did this happen?"

"During Easter break."

"That punk, Derek?"

Amanda nodded, two big tears running down her cheeks. She took her napkin and wiped her nose.

"You didn't know you were pregnant? How could you not know you were pregnant?"

I couldn't tell if Steve was raising his voice because he was angry with Amanda or with the boy. I explained why she didn't know, and told him that we only found out when she went for her school physical.

I reached over to hold Amanda's hand as she looked up at her dad and said softly, "I'm so sorry, dad."

"I'm sorry too, Amanda. I tried to protect you by getting you away from those influences, but it was too late. When's the baby due?"

"The doctor said probably in mid-January," Amanda replied.

I explained that more formal prenatal care would be necessary, and that my physician gave Amanda the contact information for a local obstetrician. Steve still looked shell-shocked.

"We'll have to make some decisions," he muttered.

I reiterated that both he and Amanda needed time to think more clearly. I also suggested that he permit Amanda to continue her plans for culinary school.

"The fall term will end in mid-December, and Amanda will have time to prepare for the baby's arrival during the holiday break."

Steve nodded, obviously mulling my words.

"Please, dad," Amanda whispered.

"We'll think about it."

Steve got up, leaned over Amanda, and embraced her. I could see Amanda shaking, as she rested her head on her dad's shoulder. Steve had tears in his eyes.

I didn't feel much like eating, but I didn't want to be rude. I took a few more bites of my sandwich, and told them I must get on the road.

As they walked me to the car, Steve again thanked me for my help, and Amanda gave me a big hug. I promised to call during the week, and noticed that they stood arm in arm as I pulled out of the driveway.

Chapter 20

I actually missed Amanda's company as I made my way to the monastery. My heart ached for her, knowing it would be such a challenging time. I prayed that her dad would be compassionate, and help her deal with all of the issues that needed to be faced.

Sister Tony was waiting when I arrived. We chatted about Amanda's summer job, and chuckled about her makeover attempts with me, but I didn't mention the recent turn of events.

"I was able to put you in the cabin closest to Betty," Tony noted as we loaded the golf cart. "The guest who was there couldn't stand the quiet, and hot-tailed it back to the city a few days early." We both laughed.

"That's great! Has Betty arrived yet?"

"She checked in earlier this afternoon. I know she's looking forward to seeing you."

Before long, I was unpacked and settled in. The cabin was identical to the one I stayed in before, though I liked the fact that it seemed to get less afternoon sun on the porch. I decided to see if Betty was at her cabin.

"Yoo Hoo," I called as I reached her front path.

Betty looked up from the book she was reading in her rocking chair.

"Ah, you made it. Come sit on the porch."

It felt good, like being with a friend I'd known for years. Betty filled me in on what she'd been working on through the last few weeks of the summer. She told me about some of the families who were down on their luck, or who had run into problems with the law.

I recognized that Betty has a special gift of always seeing the glass half-full, rather than half-empty, and I like that about her. She's no Pollyanna, and she acknowledges when there are problems, but she doesn't dwell on the negative.

I shared some stories about Amanda's adventures, especially when teaching her how to drive.

"At one point," I said, "when I was being a particularly obnoxious back-seat driver, Amanda stopped the car in the middle of the street and asked me to back off. Thank heavens there was no traffic! I learned my lesson."

We shared anecdotes for about an hour when I got a decidedly brilliant idea.

"Let's go out to eat. I know a good diner in town."

Betty's surprised look lasted only a second before she agreed wholeheartedly. We decided to freshen up, then meet at my car in the parking lot in half an hour.

Jake's Diner looked full when we arrived. Betty and I stood by the "Seat Yourself" sign, scanning the dining room for an empty table.

"Well, we now know what the locals do on Saturday night around here," Betty said.

There wasn't an empty seat in the place, except at a table for four in the back corner with one single diner. We both recognized Charlie at the same time. I decided to see if we could join him. Betty seemed reluctant, but she followed me to his little corner.

"Hi, Charlie. Would you mind if we sit here? There are no empty tables."

Charlie glanced up from his plate of meat loaf and mashed potatoes, surprised at our intrusion.

"You might remember seeing us at the monastery..."

A flash of memory lit up his eyes, and Charlie welcomed us to take a seat.

"I'm Victoria, and this is Betty."

"Nice to see you. Obviously you know that my name's Charlie."

I reminded him of the Sisters introducing us several weeks ago.

"So, you're back for another visit, huh? Of course, you're here a lot," he said to Betty.

"Just like a bad penny."

A waitress came by and added two place settings, giving us each a menu. She returned shortly with two glasses of ice water and a little bowl of lemon wedges.

I opened my menu and said, "What do you recommend, Charlie?"

"Everything's good here, but my favorites are the fish fry, the fried chicken, and the meatloaf."

I decided on the chicken with a baked potato, and Betty went for the fish fry.

"Do you come here often?" I asked.

I knew Charlie was a man of few words, but felt strange about having a side conversation with Betty when we invited ourselves to his table.

"Couple times a week."

"Sister Julie said you donate a lot of your time to help gather food for homeless shelters. How'd you get involved in that?" Betty looked at me like I had two heads.

"Guess I just noticed all the stuff they were tossing in the trash bin behind the grocery one night. Didn't seem right to me."

"I know what you mean," I said. "I figured they donated day-old food somewhere."

"Some do, but most times it just goes in the garbage. At night, homeless folks go through the trash to find something to eat. Sometimes it makes them sick."

"I never really thought about that."

"You would if you'd ever been homeless," Charlie said, as he took his last bite of meat and potatoes.

"Have you been homeless?"

"Yep."

The waitress arrived with our dinners, and Charlie asked her for a piece of coconut custard pie. My chicken was done to perfection, and I realized that I was really hungry.

Charlie must have read my expression because he smiled and said, "I told you it was good."

Betty told Charlie about her work as a public defender, and the numerous interventions she tried to make for families who were struggling.

"Sometimes people make bad decisions that get them into big trouble," Betty added.

Charlie took a bite of his pie and said, "Sometimes people don't have the things they need to make better decisions. A lot of folks are a step away from living on the street."

"I know. I met a woman whose husband divorced her for a younger model. They were pretty well to do, but he tied up their assets, and she believed she had no marketable skills to get a job. She would spend her days at the employment office and her nights sleeping in her car. One night she got mugged and was beaten up pretty bad. The police brought her to the hospital. She was out of it for a few days but, as she got better, she discovered that her wallet and credit cards had been stolen. They never found her car. She now owed the hospital thousands of dollars, and ended up on the streets."

"That's what I'm saying," Charlie said.

"What happened to her?" I asked.

"She was one of the lucky ones. I was able to help her get a job as a live-in caretaker for a cantankerous old woman, and I got the hospital administration to accept a reasonable payment plan."

"Tell me the old bag died and left her millions."

"No. Her obnoxious children grabbed every penny from the estate. Luckily, the caretaker's excellent reference got her hired as a senior helper, and she's now doing very well on her own.

"That, ladies, is what it's all about," Charlie said as he signaled for his check. "Some folks say it's not the destination that counts, but rather it's the journey. I say it's nice when the journey leads to a good destination. Now, I'd best be on my way." Charlie left a tip on the table. "You both have a nice evening."

When we arrived back at the monastery parking lot, it was quite dark. I was glad I had a flashlight in my emergency kit in the trunk of the car. We traipsed the path giggling like two schoolgirls on a late night adventure, and made plans to meet at the lake after lunch the next day.

^^^

In the morning, I called Amanda to see how she had fared her first night home. She sounded lonely and dejected, but I got her to laugh when I told her how Betty and I had intercepted Charlie's table at Jake's Diner. She said her dad wanted to hear the doctor's advice before he'd give final approval for school. In the meantime, they had made plans to practice parallel parking in the afternoon.

"Did you tell Betty about me?"

"Only how you were trying to re-make me. Actually, I was thinking it might be a good idea to get her advice. Betty has worked with a lot of families, and she may be able to offer some alternatives for you."

There was a pause as Amanda thought about my statement. "I don't care. Yeah, you can tell her."

"Have you told Kate, yet?"

"I'm not ready to tell her."

"You two talked every day, and she may be wondering why she hasn't heard from you. Besides, whatever the decision is about school will also affect Kate. I think you need to call her."

"Dad gave me my phone back."

"Then you have no excuse."

^^^

Betty was at the lake when I arrived. She laughed when she saw me with my trusty visor.

"I can see that Amanda still has her work cut out for her," she said as I spread my towel.

This time I didn't bother wearing my jeans or a shirt over my bathing suit. I kicked off my old sneakers, and put my foot into the water.

"It's still cold," I said, scrunching my nose.

"It's always cold," Betty admonished. "Let's test out the canoe."

It was still wet, so Charlie must have been fishing in the morning. We pushed the canoe into the lake until we were about knee-deep. Betty held it steady until I got settled, then she pushed off and jumped in.

"You're pretty agile for an old girl," I said.

"Speak for yourself."

Betty showed me how to paddle so I wouldn't overturn us. It wasn't long before I got the hang of it, and we both enjoyed the lull of the shimmering ripples.

"I wonder what happened to Charlie that he was homeless," I pondered aloud. "Maybe he was heartbroken when Tony left him to become a nun, so he became addicted to gambling and lost everything he owned." Betty laughed out loud.

"It's not so far-fetched," I said.

"No, unfortunately it's not. I've seen it happen, and the effects are devastating. But what makes you think it has anything to do with Tony?"

"Well, he hangs around here, and he helped her design the poustinias. Maybe Charlie decided to be like a monk, living the rest of his days in solitude."

Betty rolled her eyes and said, "Why don't you ask him?"

"Maybe I will."

We did a few more turns around the lake, and my arms were beginning to ache.

"I think I've had enough," I moaned.

Betty agreed, and we beached the canoe. We moved our towels to the shade and got comfortable.

"I called Amanda this morning."

"You miss the kid already!"

"Actually, I do. But that's not why I called her. The last couple of days have been hard on her."

"I thought she was going home to get ready for school."

"She was, but on Friday we learned that she's pregnant, and we had to tell her dad yesterday."

"Geez, why didn't you tell me?"

"She gave me permission this morning. I didn't want to betray her trust."

"How far along is she?"

"About four months. She's due in January."

"Aw, man. She was just getting her life together."

I nodded my agreement, and proceeded to tell Betty about all that had occurred the past two days.

"I'm even worried about what might happen when she tells Kate. If Amanda's dad gives her the go-ahead, will Kate still want Amanda to share an apartment? Or will the school even allow her to attend?"

"I think we're beyond those days. Still, it's not going to be easy for her."

"I just hope Amanda can continue with her plans," I said as I began gathering my things and shaking the sand from my towel. "She'll be devastated if she can't go to school with Kate. She already has enough to handle with her pregnancy."

"You heading back to your cabin?"

"Yeah. I'm going to take a little snooze. I'm getting too old for all of this excitement."

"You'd better stop saying that you're getting old. Pretty soon you're going to start believing it. Go take a nap, and I'll catch up with you later."

Chapter 21

The days passed quickly, with time for reflection, reading, and afternoon canoe rides with Betty. By mid-week, Amanda had called to say that her new obstetrician told her that the pregnancy was progressing well, and the ultrasound showed that she was having a little girl. Her dad had given his final permission for her to attend culinary school, and Kate's family was supportive of them sharing an apartment.

Though relieved, I knew it wasn't going to be easy for Amanda. The academic program was rigorous, and she'd have to be on her feet a lot. Still, Amanda assured me that she was ready.

Betty and I decided to go back to Jake's Diner for dinner on Wednesday evening. It wasn't as full as on our last visit, but it looked like the regulars were seated at the counter. We found a nice booth by the window, and Sue took our order. We both decided to try the tilapia special. I updated Betty on Amanda's news.

"My worry is that Amanda doesn't have much of a support group. None of the people who've helped her have been through what she's going to be experiencing."

"You know," Betty replied, "that's a good point. There are lots of support groups listed in the newspaper, and probably hundreds on-line. I might be able to find one that she could relate to in the city."

"I wasn't thinking of that kind of support group. But you're right. That could work. I don't want to see her alone in the city with no one to talk to."

"I think you're underestimating Amanda. From what you've told me, Kate has become a good friend and she'll be a support. Also, Amanda makes friends easily, and she'll have a lot to focus on at school. Stop being such a worry-wart. Has Amanda talked about keeping the baby?"

"She didn't mention it, and I don't think she's ready to discuss the topic."

"It's probably too soon, but I was thinking about how much I had wanted a baby. Even though I wasn't open to thinking about adoption, there are lots of women who are yearning for the opportunity to have a child."

"I know. I've seen those ads in the classifieds. But I always think they sound dubious, like some stalker lurking to steal a baby."

"They're probably legit, but there are also lots of non-profit agencies that support adoption."

"They're the kinds of things that Amanda needs to think about," I said.

"Oh, my gosh!" Betty exclaimed. What about Maggie?"

"What about her?"

"Maggie was really considering adoption the last time I spoke to her. Maybe she'd be interested in adopting Amanda's baby."

"I don't know. Don't you think it should be the other way around? Like, is Amanda interested in asking Maggie to adopt her baby?"

"Well, Amanda's probably not ready to go there. But it could be an option from either perspective. You'll know what to say when the time is right."

"I hope so."

"On another note," Betty said. "I talked to a couple of the nuns before you got to the parking lot this evening. I almost forgot to tell you."

"Tell me what?"

"The grapes are ripe," Betty said. She looked like the proverbial Cheshire cat.

"And..." I prompted.

"And I volunteered us to help with the harvesting."

"Are you kidding? When?"

"Tomorrow morning, 7:00 a.m. sharp. Meet me at the vineyards."

I groaned.

^^^

When I arrived at the vineyards, I was surprised to see so many harvesters. Charlie seemed to be supervising, and he assigned Betty and me to a row of grapevines between some of the neighboring farmhands and a couple of the Sisters. He gave us each a basket, a pair of clippers, and some directives.

Reaching in to one of the vines, Charlie showed us to look for clusters that are full, with grapes that have color and are opaque. He pinched one of the grapes and juice spurted out.

"That's what we're looking for," Charlie said.

Charlie noted that this corner of the vineyard usually ripens a week or two before the others because they had longer hours in full sun. Charlie then cupped a bunch in one hand, and used clippers to cut at the top where the cluster meets the vine. When our baskets were full, we were asked to bring them to the gathering station and take another basket.

I got the knack pretty quickly, and my basket was full in no time. Whenever I retrieved an empty basket, I felt a sense of accomplishment.

By mid-morning, Charlie called for a 15-minute break, and distributed a bottle of cold water to each of the harvesters. Most sat on the ground, trying to find some shade under the grape foliage. Betty and I joined a group of farm workers and chatted with them as we regained our energy. By the time Charlie returned with a recycling bag to collect our empty water bottles, everyone was back to work.

Betty and I egged each other on as our stamina began to waver. Neither of us was accustomed to working in the fields, and the hot, humid day did nothing to lighten the burden.

Shortly after noon, as I returned another basket to the gathering station, Charlie announced that we had accomplished our task for the day. The Sisters had prepared lunch, and we were all welcome to join them in the monastery. I waited for Betty to return her basket, and we trudged up the path together.

Wiping the sweat from my face I said, "How many baskets did you fill?"

"I lost count. How about you?"

"One more than you."

We were both laughing as we were ushered into the large, cool, dining room. The tables were pushed together to form a large U, as I imagined they might have been in the early days of the monastery. A long buffet table was set up along the wall near the kitchen, and there were a variety of sandwich fixings, as well as a hot pasta entrée. A big barrel of cold drinks was at the end of the line.

Betty and I filled our plates, grabbed two sodas, and joined some of the other workers at the table. I took a big swig before I introduced myself to those around us. Sister Tony sat to my right, Betty to my left, and Charlie plopped himself across from us.

"Well done, Charlie," Tony said.

She turned to the rest of us within earshot and added, "Our thanks to each of you. You did a fine job."

"I don't know how you folks do this, day in and day out," I said. "I'm pooped!" Everyone laughed.

A young man sitting next to Betty said, "It's hard work, but we like helping the Sisters. Plus, they pay us a fair wage and give us a nice meal."

I looked around the dining room, and watched the joyful camaraderie. Sisters sat among the field hands, and had shared in the work of the laborers. It was amazing to be a part of it all.

Toward the end of our meal, Charlie stood up and announced that the next harvest would take place the following week, same day and time. All were welcome.

As the workers began to leave, Tony thanked each of them individually, and handed each an envelope with the day's wages.

Betty and I had quietly agreed to stay and help clean up, so we remained seated. Charlie went to the barrel and brought back three cold ones.

"Thanks, Charlie. How'd you know I'd be so thirsty?"

"Just figured."

"You really are a help to the Sisters."

"They've been good to me."

"I think it goes both ways. Did you know Sister Tony before she came to the monastery?" Betty kicked me under the table.

"Guess you could say I did. Tony's my wife's sister."

I almost choked on my soda. I tried to maintain my demeanor and not seem too inquisitive.

"I didn't realize you were married, Charlie."

"I was, but my wife died a long time ago."

Charlie took a long sip of his drink. I felt a hand on my shoulder, and turned to see Sister Tony standing behind me.

"Charlie's wife was my sister, Stella. She was killed in a car accident."

"I killed her," Charlie muttered.

"Don't go there, Charlie. It wasn't your fault!"

Charlie got up from the table without another word, and walked out the door.

I apologized, and started to get up to go after him.

"Let him go, dear," Tony said softly. "Charlie has his demons and needs time alone. I'm actually surprised he told you about Stella. Even the Sisters don't know."

Tony began clearing the tables, so Betty and I joined in.

"Good going," Betty whispered.

I tried to shake my emotions as Betty and I assisted the Sisters. Two of them moved the tables to where they belonged, and others handed us clean dishes to arrange the place settings. Sister Dolores explained that the dining room was always left prepared for the next meal.

Before long, the leftovers had been put away and the kitchen was spotless. As Betty and I got ready to leave, Tony returned with an envelope for each of us.

"What's this?" Betty asked.

"It's your wages for the day." We both returned our envelopes at the same time.

"We volunteered," Betty said, "and we won't accept any payment, though we thank you for the offer. I know you can put this money to good use." I nodded in agreement.

"Let's go out to the veranda," Tony said. "The Sisters are preparing to wash the grapes, so I don't think anyone will be there."

We followed her down the hallway, and out through the French doors to the screened porch. It was still warm, but a nice breeze wafted through.

"I think I owe you an explanation."

I protested, saying it was none of my business.

"Nonsense. Charlie began to tell you about Stella, and I interrupted. I apologize."

Sister Tony looked out over the vineyards, seeming to gather her thoughts.

After a few moments, she said, "Stella was a year older than I and, although she was much more headstrong, we were very close. When she was 19, she met Charlie Munley at a party for one of her friends. He, too, was 19 and worked as a stockboy at the local hardware store. Stella fell in love with him and, despite my parents' objections, they eloped. As you can imagine, that caused a lot of tension in our family. Mom and Dad thought they were too young to marry, and they didn't think that Charlie would be able to support Stella. In less than a year, Stella and Charlie had a baby, a little boy they named Aaron."

"Aaron was a darling with big brown eyes and a smile that could light the world. When he was about a year old, the three of them were driving home from a friend's house. They rounded a bend in the road, and suddenly saw a pick-up truck weaving into their lane at a high speed. Charlie tried to swerve to the left to avoid an accident, but the truck smashed into the passenger side. Stella died instantly."

Tony took a deep breath. "The truck driver died, too. Toxicology results indicated a high level of alcohol and drugs in his blood. Charlie had a broken leg. I don't know how he managed, but he got Aaron out of his car seat and away from the wreck."

"Oh, my gosh," I managed to whisper.

Tony seemed lost in a distant world. "At the funeral, my parents wouldn't even acknowledge Charlie. They blamed him for Stella's death, although it clearly wasn't his fault. After the burial, Charlie walked away and disappeared from our lives. The next time I saw him was when he came to the monastery to find me, thirty years later."

"What happened to the baby?"

"Charlie said that he couldn't care for him. He put little Aaron up for adoption, then spiraled into a deep depression."

"Charlie told me he'd been homeless."

"Yes, he lived on the street, picking up odd jobs, always moving on."

"Did he know you had joined the monastery?"

"I didn't enter the community until a few years after Stella's death. Years later, he saw an article about the winery with my picture. We had returned to our family names by then, so he came looking for me."

"Did you recognize him after all those years?" Betty asked.

"Oh, yes. Even though his thick hair had turned white and his eyes had lost their twinkle, I knew it was Charlie the minute I saw him. We had quite a tearful reunion."

Tony faltered, obviously reflecting back to that day. Then she continued her story.

"When Charlie told me about his personal circumstances, I offered him a job tending the gardens. Over time, we began to plan the cabins, and the Sisters liked the idea of him living in one of them. I think it gave us all a sense of security."

"I can understand that," I remarked. "But doesn't he get lonely and bored living in the woods?"

"I'm sure you've noticed that Charlie's a private person, and the lifestyle here suits him. But I've seen him grow much more open in the last year or so. It's as if he's finding his spirit again."

"I think you and the Sisters have helped him immensely," Betty noted. "It's amazing that he's beginning to come out of the darkness after all he's been through."

"And he's helped us so much," Tony said. "It's such a blessing to have him here."

I could sense that it was time to leave. I gave Tony a hug, and told her that I was grateful to have experienced this day.

Tony thanked us again as she led us to the door. Betty and I walked back to our cabins, both of us enveloped in our own thoughts.

Chapter 22

After a long, hot shower and a good night's sleep, I awoke refreshed and ready for a new day. It was good to have worked in the vineyards the day before. I felt as if I were an integral part of this serving community.

I took a cup of tea out to the porch and mulled over what had brought me here, and what I had garnered over the last few months. My soul had been yearning for new spirit and energy. I would never have expected to find it, or whatever I was feeling, in a cabin on the grounds of a monastery.

My musings were interrupted by Charlie coming up the path with two very ripe tomatoes.

"Good morning, Victoria. I've come to apologize to you, and give you a peace offering."

I accepted his gifts graciously, trying not to squish them, and I placed them gently on the little table.

"No apology's necessary, Charlie. I was out of line for prying. Would you like a cup of tea?"

"No, ma'am, but thanks. You know, I thought I could answer your questions yesterday. I felt kind of safe, if you know what I mean."

"I think I do. I feel comfortable talking to you, too."

"Did you ever have anything happen to you in life that changed everything?" Charlie asked.

I thought back over the years.

"I guess I did," I said slowly.

"Like what?"

Now look who was asking the probing questions.

"I guess the biggest challenge came from losing a man I truly loved. I had thought that we would marry and raise a family, but he moved away and married someone else. Not having any children was also a big loss to me. I guess after that I just played it safe."

"Losing someone you love is a powerful loss. In my case, not only did I lose my darling Stella, but I gave away my boy, Aaron." Charlie cleared his throat, choking back deep emotion. "That's the first time I ever said those words out loud."

"Do you want to tell me about it?"

Charlie looked out into the woods, then his words began to take shape. He recounted his story, a rendition that echoed Tony's words from the day before. As Charlie told it, however, I could feel his depth of despair, and the huge void that had filled his being and took away his spirit. Tears welled in my eyes.

"I'm so sorry," I said softly.

"When I came here," Charlie said, "I found the peace that I'd been searching for. I must have been crazy to give up Aaron. He was my only connection to Stella until I found Tony. But I couldn't take care of him. I tried, but with my broken leg, I could barely get around, and he cried constantly for his mother. I left town because Stella's family blamed me for her death. I had no family, no job, and no money. A few weeks later, when Aaron got a fever, I took him to Suburban Hospital, and told them to find a good home for him. I'll regret it every day of my life."

"Did you ever try to find Aaron?

"No. I started to drink heavily and lived hand to mouth. It took me awhile to get sober and clean up my act. By then, it was too late to go looking for him. I just hope that he turned out all right."

"You know, Charlie. I remember reading that it's not until we're lost that we begin to find ourselves. Despite all you've been through, you've been transformed into someone far greater than you would have been without the adversity you experienced."

"Sounds to me like a bunch of crap, but I know what you're trying to say. One of these days I may believe it. Now, I'd best be getting to my chores. I told the Sisters that I'd be there to give a hand with the grapes we picked yesterday."

"Do they need any other help?"

"Don't think so. I just lend my muscles for the heavy lifting." He flexed his arms and added, "You were a great help yesterday."

"I have to admit that I was pretty tired last night. I now have a much greater appreciation for those who work outside in the heat and humidity."

Charlie agreed, noting that the pay isn't that great for farm laborers either.

As he got ready to leave, Charlie said, "I'm planning to eat at Jake's Diner tonight. If you and Betty don't have any plans, why don't you join me? I figure I'll be there by 6 p.m."

I told Charlie that I'd see Betty at the lake after lunch, and I felt sure she'd enjoy going to Jake's place.

"We can't dawdle," Charlie said as he stepped off the porch. "I call Bingo at the Fire House at 7 p.m.

^ ^ ^

One of the other guests was paddling the canoe around the lake, so Betty and I sat on the beach watching him. He was pretty good at it, I had to admit. I told Betty about Charlie's visit, and that we'd be meeting him at Jake's Diner for supper. I figured if she could volunteer me to pick grapes, I could get her to do dinner. I wasn't so sure about the Bingo thing. That might take some convincing.

"Are you sure you want me to tag along?"

"What's that supposed to mean? Charlie specifically invited both of us. Besides, he'll be leaving to call Bingo at 7 p.m."

"Uh huh. And, I guess you want to go to Bingo?"

"I thought it might be fun. Who knows, we might win something." Betty rolled her eyes.

"I guess it wouldn't hurt," Betty said. "It's not like I have a full social calendar this week. So, why did Charlie visit you this morning?"

I explained that he came to apologize for walking out the day before.

"He told me his story."

"Wow! He must really trust you. Was it the same as the one Tony told us?"

"Basically, but deeper, with more raw emotion. He's still mourning the loss of his wife, and I think he terribly regrets giving his son up for adoption."

"That's not unusual," Betty said. "He might have felt that he had no other option at the time." I nodded my agreement. "The boy must be grown up and on his own now. I wonder if Charlie's ever tried to find him. Of course, that probably would depend on whether or not it was an open adoption."

"He said he didn't," I said. "I think he figures what's done is done. He knew he couldn't care for the boy, but I don't know that he ever expected the depth of despair he experienced. Besides, how would he ever find Aaron now? He must be at least 40 years old."

"He'd have to begin with the agency that processed the adoption."

"He didn't take the boy to an agency. He took him to a hospital."

"There still has to be a paper trail. There are also lawyers and private investigators who specialize in adoption searches."

"This is one of the reasons I want Amanda to explore all of her options before she decides what to do about the baby," I said. "I don't want her to make a rash decision while she's still emotionally upset, nor do I want to see anyone push her into a decision she's not ready to make."

Betty agreed, but reminded me that adoption is the right choice if someone doesn't have the resources to care for a child.

Betty and I chatted like two best friends, sharing tidbits of our lives as if we were catching up from long ago. We seemed to share similar interests, despite our different backgrounds. I liked her funny quips and wise insights.

Occasionally, we would glance at the rhythmic ripples on the lake, generated by the even rowing strokes of the guest in the canoe. Eventually the sun and gentle cadence of the water worked their magic on both of us, and we decided it was time to head back to our cabins to take a little snooze before our night on the town.

Shaking the sand from our towels, I asked Betty if she had met the guy in the canoe. I noted that I hadn't ever seen him before.

"I think he might have just arrived today. I've seen him here before, but I don't remember his name. He keeps pretty much to himself. Seems to me that he comes for long weekends if there's an available cabin."

"I'm going to wave to Mr. Canoe Man," I told Betty.

"I doubt that Mr. Canoe Man is interested in two chatty broads flirting with him. Let's go."

As we got to the copse of trees, I suddenly turned, gave him my most alluring pose, and waved. Betty grabbed my arm, pulled me into the woods, and cracked up laughing.

"What did he do," she giggled.

Smugly I said, "He waved back."

^ ^ ^

Our dinner with Charlie was interesting. He's not a big talker, but he's relaxed in his own environment. He ordered his usual meatloaf and mashed potatoes, and was intent on eating while Betty and I chatted through our meal. I interrupted his musings by asking about Mr. Canoe Man.

"That's Jeff Stodges. He's CEO of some big company in the city. He worked out an arrangement with Tony that if a cabin becomes available on a weekend, she could call him on short notice."

"That seems like an extra burden on the Sisters. Someone has to clean the cabins twice in one week."

"I'm the one who takes care of the cabins, and I don't mind at all. It's extra revenue for the nuns, and he's the guy who donated the canoe and screen doors. Besides that, he's a pretty nice guy."

Charlie sure could talk when he wanted to. I decided to press forward, despite Betty kicking my foot under the table.

"So, what's his story?"

Charlie mounded some mashed potatoes onto a piece of meatloaf and forked it into his mouth. I kicked Betty back while we waited for Charlie's response.

"I don't know what you mean by a story."

"Come on, Charlie. Everyone's got a story."

"Like what?"

"You live here because you found peace and acceptance," I began. "Betty comes here to escape from her hectic pace, and it brings memories of her deceased husband." I was just getting started. "Amanda was sent here by her father to get her away from the dysfunctional influences of her friends. Maggie was running away from her husband who wouldn't communicate with her, and didn't understand her need to have a baby."

As I paused to collect my thoughts, Charlie prompted, "And what's your story, Victoria?"

"Me? I don't have a story." Betty burst out laughing.

"Sure you do," Charlie said. "Everyone has a story."

"OK, I saw a brochure for this place on a bulletin board at the post office. I was in a long line, so I read about it, and I was intrigued."

"That's not your story, Victoria. That's how you discovered the monastery. What's your story?"

I pushed the peas around my plate. I hate peas. I looked directly at Charlie. His hazel eyes were deep chasms of mesmerizing clearness. I imagined that they were once pools of darkness.

"I don't know, Charlie. I'm not sure where I've been or where I'm headed."

"Then that's your story. You're here to discover who you are and what you're meant to be."

Charlie ordered a piece of pie, while I mulled over his words. The conversation did not go in the direction I had planned. Betty made small talk while Charlie wiped his mouth and said, "I've got to go ladies. It's Bingo night. Are you planning to join me at the Fire House?"

Chapter 23

I had fun last night, I mused as I sipped my morning tea on the porch. I didn't do too badly at Bingo. Winning $25 on a pull-tab paid for my games. I smiled when I thought about Betty's excited yell of "Bingo!" Charlie patiently checked each of the numbers Betty called off, and declared her the winner of $200.

I watched a little chipmunk scurry among the shrubs. He found his buddy and they chased each other around the trees. Their carefree banter made me think of Charlie's comment to me during last evening's supper conversation. Was he teasing or was he challenging me to think beyond my normal boundaries? What brought me here to the poustinias at this time of my life? What is my story?

On the surface, it seemed as simple as looking at a brochure in the post office. What made me call a monastery to reserve a cabin in the middle of nowhere? What drew me back, luring me into harvesting grapes in a hot field, chatting with nuns and migrant works—none of whom I would normally associate with. Charlie suggested that my story was of self-discovery. How ridiculous is that? I should have told him I'm a respected businesswoman with many accomplishments. He probably thinks I'm just some old dowager whose heart was hardened after being jilted in love.

My reverie was making me grumpy. I decided to call Myra and check on Harvey. Myra picked up on the second ring. "Well, it's about time, neighbor!" she said as the call connected.

"You don't know how busy I've been."

"Well, your boy has been missing you, but he's settled in nicely. I think he likes it here." Darn traitor. How could Harvey be settling in with Myra?

Myra proceeded to tell me that Amanda and Kate were becoming the best of friends. They had both stopped by to see her during the week, and Amanda told her of her pregnancy.

"I felt so sad for her," Myra said. "This should be a time of joy, but she has to deal with all of the challenges of nurturing a child while she goes to school and begins life on her own."

"Did she seem overwhelmed when you saw her?"

"Didn't seem like it. She said she's been feeling lots of emotions, but her dad told her that she could go on with her plans."

"That's good. It sounds like he's being supportive."

"No doubt, he is. Amanda was surprised at how helpful he's been once he got over his first shock. I can only imagine how my son would react if Kate came home with such news."

Myra told me that the girls were moving into their apartment near the school in two days. They were busy shopping for some furnishings, and garnering all the stored items they could find from their parents' attics. Knowing Amanda, she'd be adding her decorating touch to make their little place a home.

"What time do you plan to be home tomorrow?"

"I'm not sure. I'm thinking of staying another week if you can still dog-sit for me."

Where in the world did that come from? Silence on the other end of the line indicated that Myra was thinking the same thing.

"Of course I can still watch Harvey. But what's going on? I don't think you've taken a decent vacation in years. Now you're working on the third week this summer in a rustic cabin. Are you OK?"

"I'm better than OK. I'm great! In fact, I feel more alive than I have in years."

"Maybe you've been imbibing too much of the nuns' wine," Myra teased.

"Not even a taste," I said with a chuckle. "But, speaking of the nuns, I'd better check to see if my cabin is available for next week. I'll get back to you when I've worked out the details."

∧∧∧

I met Betty at the lake after lunch as we had planned the night before. She was already settled in her spot on the sand.

"You're looking mighty chipper today," Betty said. "How about a canoe ride to celebrate our last day?"

"I thought for sure Mr. Canoe Man would be out on the lake."

"Oh, he was. He spent the morning fishing, and he's going to take a nap this afternoon. He plans to go in town for dinner."

"Whoa! It sounds like you've been flirting with Mr. Canoe Man!"

"Not at all! ...Well, maybe just a little bit," she said as she pulled me toward the canoe.

We pushed the canoe into the water, then managed to get ourselves settled without overturning. It wasn't long before we were gliding smoothly across the lake.

"OK, spill the beans," I said.

"Nothing to spill. I was just being neighborly."

Betty recounted that she had met Jeff on her morning walk, and they had chatted for about an hour before he went to get his fishing gear. She just happened to go to the beach earlier than usual, and they ended up talking for another hour after he beached the canoe.

"Did he catch any fish?"

"I don't know. I didn't notice."

"So what did you learn about Mr. Canoe Man?" I asked.

"Jeff?"

"Yes, Jeff." I rolled my eyes.

"Oh, we didn't talk too much about personal stuff. We discussed our work, why we like coming to the monastery, where we like to travel. You know, just plain old neighborly conversation."

"How old is he?"

"I'm guessing he's probably in his late 50's or early 60's. Handsome guy."

"Well, too bad you're leaving tomorrow." We stopped rowing and allowed the canoe to drift.

"No problem. We're going out to dinner tonight and I'll give him my phone number."

I laughed so hard that I almost tipped the canoe.

"What's so funny? I'm just being neighborly!"

"Uh huh."

We worked to settle the canoe. Eventually, we got into a rowing cadence again, and I told Betty of my plans to stay another week. Her eyes opened wide, a combination of surprise and questioning. I explained how the idea had come to me suddenly when I was talking to Myra, and that Tony said she could make the arrangements. My secretary would hold down the fort at the firm.

"I'm just not ready to leave."

"I understand. You've been bitten by the poustinia bug. I wish I could stay, too, but I have a few scheduled court cases I can't miss."

"I wish you could stay as well. I enjoy your company. Do you know that this week I didn't even make a schedule?"

"We were too busy to follow a schedule."

"We were. But it's so un-like me! I always plan my day."

"So what are you going to do next week?"

"I don't know. I'm just going to let it unfold."

Chapter 24

I was beginning to second guess my decision to stay another week when Betty pulled out of the parking lot the next day. Suddenly I felt alone, somewhat like my first day when I stepped into the unknown at the Monastery of St. Carmella.

As I trudged back to the cabin, I smiled at the memory of Betty's tale of her dinner with Jeff. As usual, they had gone to Jake's Diner. Surprisingly, it really is the only eatery within a reasonable distance, and they serve good food.

Betty and Jeff chatted easily on the short drive. As they slid into a booth, Betty noticed the wedding band on Jeff's left ring finger. Jeff explained that he and his wife have been married for 31 years and, though they share a lot of interests, they have very different personalities. He likes to unwind in peace and quiet; she's energized by a crowd.

The arrangement that Jeff has with the monastery works out perfectly for both of them. When Sister Tony calls to say there's a cabin available for the weekend, Jeff gets to relax with nature, while his wife has a weekend with the girls.

I thought Betty would be disappointed about Jeff's unavailability, but she said they had an enjoyable conversation, and he was quite interested in providing internships for some of the teens she worked with.

I decided to give Amanda a call while I rested on my porch stoop. I had refrained from calling all week as I knew that she had her obstetrician appointment, and she was busy moving into her new place. She seemed delighted to hear my voice and said it was perfect timing since she and Kate had just taken a break from unpacking more boxes.

Amanda sounded exuberant, a far cry from when I left her at her dad's house a week ago. She reiterated a lot of what Myra had shared with me, especially that her dad had been awesome. She liked the obstetrician, who told her that she was definitely made for making babies, and was in the perfect weight range for this stage of gestation. Kate, too, was awesome. For that matter, everyone had been awesome.

School was beginning on Wednesday and Amanda couldn't wait to meet the other students in her class. There was going to be an orientation party on Tuesday evening, and she and Kate were helping each other pick out the most appropriate, cool, and trendy outfits. They, too, were going to be awesome.

Amanda didn't seem too surprised that I planned to stay another week at the poustinia. She hoped I was continuing to loosen up. That's what she said—loosen up! So, I told her I wasn't even making a daily schedule these days. She suggested that I might want to head to the outlet mall and get a few wild outfits and some body piercings. We both laughed.

"I promise," I told her as we bid our farewells, "the next time I see you, you'll be amazed at my transformation!"

On that note, I grabbed my visor, sunscreen, book, and towel for my trek to the lake. Charlie was fishing from the raft when I arrived, and I settled myself on the sand. I was fully engrossed in my novel when I heard the scrunch of the canoe on the sand.

"Did you catch anything, Charlie?"

I looked up, squinting with the sun.

"A couple of runts I threw back. Might as well let them get a tad bigger so the nuns can have a nice fish dinner."

Charlie maneuvered the canoe out of the water.

"I thought you'd be cleaning cabins today."

Charlie let out a big guffaw!

"I think I might have misled you, Victoria. I don't do the cleaning. Your rental fee covers the cost of a service. I do check to make sure that the cabins are ready for new guests. Guess I won't have to worry about yours this week. I hear you've extended your visit."

"You know," Charlie continued hesitantly, "Victoria is a pretty name, but it sounds so formal—like a queen, if you know what I mean." We both laughed at his unexpected rhyme.

"Do you mind if I call you Vicki? I think it fits you better."

"No problem," I responded, and then chuckled.

I explained that Amanda had told me that she hoped I'd loosen up this week.

"You've helped me take a giant leap towards her imposed goal, Charlie."

"Glad to be obliged, Vicki. I take it that Amanda's the kid whose father dropped off here earlier this summer. Tony told me you took her in, gave her job and all."

"I think it was good for both of us. Misguided as it might have been, her dad was just trying to remove her from dysfunctional influences. Unfortunately, he was too late."

Uh-oh. Even my tongue was becoming loose.

"I know. Tony told me she got pregnant. Her dad called to ask the Sisters for prayers. I guess she's starting culinary school this week. Moved in with a nice girl she met when she was staying with you."

At least I wasn't the one who let the cat out of the bag, but word travels fast around these parts.

"Kate's sweet, and they both have similar interests. I feel certain that Amanda's going to be fine. By the way, Charlie, one of the reasons I stayed is because I want to help with the grape harvesting this week."

"Great! I'll put you on my list of volunteers. Maybe while you're here I can show you some of the birdhouses I make in my spare time."

"That's cool. What kind of birdhouses do you make?"

"I like making little buildings—you know, like houses and barns, things like that. I put a little hole and perch in the front, and the roof has hinges so I can easily add the feed. This spring I had a bunch of baby birds, mostly starlings and wrens. I think the starlings like to nest here so they can be close to the vineyards. They like to eat insects and fruit. The wrens go after the insects, and I guess the lake is a good breeding ground for mosquitoes. There's plenty of natural food around here, though I still like to fill their houses with wild seed."

"I don't think I'd know the difference between starlings and wrens," I chuckled.

"Oh, they're very different. And you'd definitely know when you hear a wren. They sing very loudly."

"Do you make your birdhouses in town?"

"Nope. Right here in my little poustinia. I do sell them in town, though. Never thought I'd make any money on them, but I've got a little business going. Well, at least I make enough that I can buy wood and paint."

"That's amazing! But how do you cut the wood? Don't tell me you have a power saw in your cabin!" We both laughed.

"Nah, I don't think Tony would go for me disturbing the peace. One of my buddies at the Fire House cuts my wood. I give him the dimensions, buy him a few donuts, and take my supplies back to the cabin where I can work in the evenings. You'll have to come and visit so you can see some of my designs.

"I'd love to see your birdhouses, Charlie. When you have some free time, stop by and we can walk over to your place."

"That sounds like a plan. Now I've got to go check on the cabins. You have a nice evening."

I watched Charlie pull the canoe to its resting place. He really wasn't as old as I had first thought. His thick white hair and ruddy tan make him appear more aged, but he's quite trim and agile. I was pleasantly surprised that he had such an interesting hobby, and even had buddies in town. First impressions are not always reliable.

I shook my towel to shed its sand and picked up my book. As I walked back to the cabin, I thought about how much I enjoyed the new people in my life. I felt a more carefree me emerging from somewhere deep inside. It was a strange feeling.

^^^

After supper, I took a walk toward the monastery. The setting sun illuminated the beautiful stone structure, and highlighted the various stained glass windows. I could imagine the pride of a community—not just the Sisters who committed their lives to service and prayer, but also the farmers and townspeople who basked in its strength and tranquility.

I noticed Sister Tony helping a new guest load up his gear into the golf cart. It looked like he was planning to camp for a month! Was that a charcoal grill he was squeezing into the back of the cart? I waved, but they were deeply engrossed. He was definitely a newbie. In my musing, I nearly collided with Sister Julie and Sister Dolores who were also chuckling at the scene in the parking lot.

"I give him two days," Julie bantered.

"Looks to me like he's planning to stay awhile," Dolores countered. "My money's on four days!"

I joined strides with the nuns who invited me to stroll with them. They told me that they had heard I was staying another week, and that I'd be helping with the next grape harvest.

"Take advantage of it while you can, Victoria," Dolores said. "We may be closing our doors by the end of the year."

I think I saw Julie nudge her.

"You seem like part of the family," Julie noted, "but we shouldn't burden you with our problems."

Nuns have problems? Who would guess?

"It seems like you have a steady stream of guests. Why would you go out of business?"

"The poustinias have been a good source of revenue, and our wine sales have been steady, but we just don't have the numbers of Sisters available to warrant keeping this big old mansion. Many of the younger sisters have been assigned to study or to work in the missions. The higher ups are considering a merger with another branch of our Sisters in the mid-west, so we probably will all be reassigned."

We rested at two park benches nestled by one of the gardens overlooking the vineyards. I pondered their words. The sky had a beautiful pink hue as the sun slipped further on the horizon. Tony returned from her delivery, parked the golf cart on the side of the road, and joined us.

"I'm getting too old for all of this," she said as she sat down. I noticed how tired she looked. The dark circles under her eyes betrayed recent sleepless nights and deep worry.

I shared that we had been discussing the turn of events that could impact the survival of the monastery. Tony's smile turned to chagrin, but she kept her composure.

"The Sisters in administration have to make decisions that will benefit the survival of our community."

"I recognize that I have no knowledge of how the sisterhood functions, and certainly it's none of my business. However, I can't fathom that it doesn't operate much differently than any organization. You need a group of people who have a united vision, an administrative team to provide direction, and enough financial resources to maintain the goals of the mission."

I could see that the Sisters were mulling my words.

"On the surface," I continued, "the Monastery of St. Carmella could seem like an albatross. The majority of the Sisters here are in the infirmary, and I'm sure it takes a lot of money to heat and cool the mansion. On the other hand, these stone walls hold many memories for the nuns who got their training here, who worked in the vineyards, and who buried their elders in the cemetery out back."

"Memories don't count, Victoria," Tony said.

"Memories do count in an organization that's mission-driven, not business-driven. But I don't disagree that you need to make wise financial decisions. You've tried to do that, Tony, by continuing to harvest the vineyard, make the wine, and build the poustinias."

"It's not enough. We don't even have sufficient Sisters to make the wine any more. Production is outsourced, though they use our recipes, and we receive income from the sales."

"That, too, was a wise decision. You could have let the grape vines go fallow. Don't be so hard on yourself."

"That's right," Julie said. "If we had no grapes, I wouldn't be able to make my batches of grape jelly!"

"I bet your jelly's delicious!" I said. "I hope I'll get a chance to try some." I noticed that dusk was descending. "On that note, I'd better get back to my cabin before I can't find my way in the darkness."

The Sisters bid good night blessings. Before we departed, they invited me to their Labor Day cookout. I told them I'd be delighted to come. Then I added, "And get some sleep, Tony. You're looking mighty tired these days."

Chapter 25

I didn't get much sleep myself. When I got back to the cabin, I made some tea, and got out my notepad and pen. I always do my best thinking with pen and paper.

I tried to conjecture what I'd do if I were part of the nun administration. That wasn't so easy, as I had no point of reference. Nuns pray and do good work. That's all well and good, but my direction kept leading to blind alleys, like maze puzzles. The thing about mazes, I thought, is that it's easy to get lost, but there's always a way out.

I decided to list pros and cons, trying to put together my thoughts from a nun's perspective. I chuckled at the vision of me in nunly garb with a veil to cover my hair.

By midnight, and a number of cups of tea later, I had a fairly decent collection of factors that would influence decisions about the monastery, but nothing that gave me clear direction.

I placed my mug in the sink, got ready for bed, and turned out the light. Too much caffeine and an overactive mind had me tossing and turning for most of the night.

The ringtone on my phone brought me out of a deep sleep. I glanced at my watch and saw that the morning was well past its prime. Betty chuckled at my groggy hello.

"Don't tell me I woke you up! I know it's Labor Day, but it's not like you to sleep away the day."

I told Betty about my discussion with the Sisters last evening, and my work far into the night.

"It's not your problem."

"I know it's not, but if you saw how exhausted Tony looked…"

"And now you're in the same boat."

I admitted that Betty was right.

"Now, get up, get dressed, and get moving," she chanted like a drill sergeant. "And call me back later if you feel like chatting."

I put on my bathing suit, and meandered through the trees to the lake. The day was becoming oppressively hot and humid, and not even a whisper of a breeze moved the foliage. When I arrived, Charlie was fishing, and the newbie was floating on an inflatable raft with a beer in-hand. Two other guests were out in the canoe.

I spread my towel on the sandy beach, and kicked off my sneakers. The shimmering lake beckoned to me. I tested the water with my bare feet, then went a little farther.

Little by little, my body adjusted to the cold water, and I continued until the ripples reached my shoulders. My toes squished in the slimy mud on the bottom of the lake, and I went all-in.

I gasped at the initial chill, until I felt exhilarated. I gauged the distance, and decided to swim to the anchored dock. Charlie had apparently seen me coming, and had taken his line out of the water. He helped me up the side ladder.

"Wow! That felt good," I said, slightly out of breath.

"You swim pretty good," Charlie commented with a smile.

"I'd take a heated pool any day, but today the lake feels great!"

Charlie beckoned me to sit on the edge of the platform, with my legs dangling in the water. We watched as an egret made landing on the sandy beach across the lake. There was a comfortable silence between us as we observed the tranquility of nature unfolding.

"Tony told me about last evening's conversation when I was weeding the gardens this morning."

"I know… It's none of my business."

"Not mine either. The Sisters will do what they have to do. Still, Tony's my sister-in-law, and I can see the toll of all this worry. I've tried to help in my own way, but that doesn't go very far in resolving the problem."

I reassured Charlie that the monastery doors might have closed years ago had he not reunited with his wife's sister. He nodded in agreement while we both continued to gaze across the water.

"You think we ought to stay out of it?" Charlie asked.

"Yeah."

"I don't know if I can," Charlie muttered. I turned to look at him.

"I don't know if I can either."

I suddenly felt as if we were kindred spirits, conniving against the powers that be.

"I was awake half the night, trying to come up with a solution," I said.

"Any ideas?"

"Not yet, but the cold swim cleared my brain."

"Maybe we could work on it together. I've learned a lot about how the Sisters operate, and I know this place like the back of my hand."

"I think we'd make a pretty good team."

Charlie smiled and slid his body into the water. I gasped as I did the same.

"I'll race you to the beach!" he challenged.

Charlie was barely winded when he reached the shore ahead of me. While I caught my breath and put on my sneakers, he suggested that we take a walk to his place so I could see his birdhouses. I grabbed my towel, and followed him along the wooded path.

I was amazed at the beautiful artistry and various designs of the birdhouses scattered among the trees and shrubs surrounding Charlie's cabin. Some were hanging on tree branches, while a few were perched atop poles near the garden. Each was unique.

One was a replica of the poustinia, including a little front porch. There was a log cabin, a red barn, a winter chalet, and even a small rendition of the monastery. Charlie explained the inspiration for each of his creations as we walked around the yard.

"This one's a big seller in town," he said as he pointed to a little farmhouse. "If you look in the little window, you can still see the starling nest."

"Oh, how cute! These are wonderful, Charlie!"

"You want to come in and see the one I'm working on now?"

The inside of Charlie's cabin was the same as all of the others, except that he had a larger square table instead of a desk in the corner. Shelves lined the two walls abutting the table, and they were stacked with plastic shoe boxes, each labeled and filled with tools and paints. I could see that Charlie had been painting various pieces of wood, and they were spread out on the table to dry.

"This one's going to be a replica of the Fire House," Charlie noted. "It's a little more challenging because I'm making it two stories high. I'm putting a large bay doorway on the lower level of the front, like where the fire engine would go, and a little pole up to the second floor where the birds can feed. The roof will open on hinges for adding the bird seed."

"Wow! I'm speechless! You have such a great talent, Charlie! I hope I get to see the finished product. How long's it take to build a birdhouse?"

"This one'll take a few weeks, especially now that we're in the grape harvesting season. The smaller ones that I sell only take me a few days to finish. I make a lot of them in the winter."

"Did you know you had such a flair for design? What made you decide to build birdhouses?"

"When I was doing odd jobs, always on the move before I came here, I often worked in carpentry. Then, when I suggested the cabins to Tony, she let me build this one as the prototype. She gave them the fancy religious name of poustina—a private place of prayer. Anyway, I knew I liked building things, and birdhouses were easy enough to create in this small space. I just never imagined that I could make a business of it."

"It's wonderful, Charlie. Thanks so much for showing me your creations. I can't tell you how impressed I am! Now I'd better let you have some time to get ready for the Sisters' barbecue. I have a feeling that you help them with the celebration."

"I man the grill," Charlie chuckled. "I hope you plan on being there."

"I wouldn't miss it," I said as I opened the screen door. "See you later!"

^^^

When I got back to my cabin, I took a shower and put on a pair of red shorts and a white top with red and blue diagonal stripes. I laid on the bed and returned Betty's call. I told her that I had braved the cold lake and had a refreshing swim, and she laughed at my description of the newbie who was taking the poustinias to a whole new level.

I also mentioned that I had visited Charlie's cabin to see his birdhouses. She seemed surprised that Charlie was becoming so sociable. Betty told me that she planned to join some friends for a Labor Day cookout, and I told her that the Sisters had invited me to theirs. By the end of our conversation, my eyelids had a weight of their own, and I fell fast asleep.

I awoke just in time to walk to the monastery for the festivities. Barbecue aromas were wafting from the garden behind the screened porch. Several picnic tables had been decorated with patriotic covers, and a buffet table had platters of salads, condiments, and desserts. I wasn't too surprised to see Charlie basting ribs on the grill.

"You're just in time to help me bring out the corn and potato salad, Victoria," Tony said.

I followed her into the kitchen where Julie and Dolores were dishing out the last of the picnic foods. They handed me a big bowl of farm-fresh corn on the cob, and told me to ask Charlie if he was ready for the hamburgers and hot dogs.

A couple of the nuns and one of the guests had seated themselves at a picnic table, and Tony was making plates for some of the older Sisters from the infirmary who had been brought to the porch. I didn't see the newbie. I guess he had his own barbecue at the poustinia.

I brought out the hamburgers and hot dogs for Charlie, and handed him a cold soda. He looked like he needed one. By the time I delivered a platter of grilled meats to the buffet table, I realized that I hadn't eaten all day.

It was a delightful and care-free picnic. The Sisters told stories of their early days at the monastery, and recounted some of their shenanigans when they were novices. Tony shared that she had tried to sneak in a rum cake from her parents on a visitation day, but had been caught hiding it on the back stairs. Julie noted that she and a couple of the young Sisters snuck into the kitchen in the middle of the night and had a party of sodas and Little Debbie cakes.

"Did you get caught?"

"No, but I was as sick as a dog the next day."

One of the nuns on the porch called out, "Don't think we didn't know about that party!" Everyone cracked up laughing.

By the time the mosquitoes began nipping and dusk was arriving, everyone helped take platters back to the kitchen. As I walked back to my cabin, I reflected on the spirit of community and hospitality that the nuns shared. Not only did they have a bond of sisterhood, but they also welcomed others to share in their joyfulness.

Chapter 26

The next morning, I added my reflections about the spirit of the Sisters to my notes from the previous evening. Some ideas were beginning to take shape, as I saw threads of commonality in my thoughts. I wanted to get feedback from Charlie, so I put on my bathing suit and headed for the lake. He wasn't there.

Later at my cabin, Charlie stopped by with a couple of apples he had left over from his delivery of food for the poor. I showed him my notes, and suggested that we could see if anything credible might emerge that would help the Sisters. I think Charlie felt a bit awkward standing on my porch, but he didn't want to come in.

"How about we have dinner at Jake's Diner in an hour or so," Charlie suggested. I agreed and said I'd meet him there.

"No reason for both of us to use our gas. I can drive. I'll meet you at the parking lot at 6 p.m. Bring your notebook."

"Sounds like a plan," I said. Charlie did a little jig off the steps.

It didn't take long to get to the diner. Charlie waved to a few of his cronies as we slid into a booth. In a matter of minutes, we placed our orders, and I opened my notebook.

"I've been doing some thinking, Vicki. First of all, the nuns are going to do what they have to do. They take a vow of obedience, so they don't have much choice. That being said, Tony has a streak of stubbornness in her. Runs in her family. She wouldn't take much of us coming in and telling her what we think she should do. It's got to be her idea."

"That's helpful to know. Are you any good at making Tony think something's her idea?"

"Yep, pretty good, if I may say so myself."

"That's what I was thinking. Whatever we come up with has to fit with who they are and what they do. I got a sense of that last night at the barbecue and last week at the harvest. The Sisters have a spirit of joy and hospitality. They look out for each other, and are respectful of their land. They help their neighbors, provide jobs for the poor, and even educate those who come from another culture who may stay in the farm community for only a short time. The nuns also manage their resources well. Revenue from the winery and the poustinias has kept them afloat, even though the number of Sisters at the monastery has continued to decline."

"Darn sure. Tony's been a driving force for all of that."

"I think you've played a role, too," I replied as the waitress brought our food. My words didn't go unnoticed, even though Charlie began dousing his fries with ketchup.

"Do any of the Sisters come to the poustinias for retreat?"

"I think there've been a few through the years."

"Why only a few?"

"Guess because they needed money from paying guests."

"Did they market to the Sisters?"

"I don't know. Why?"

"Apparently, they may merge with a larger bunch of their community from the mid-west. If those Sisters have never seen this place, they'd probably make a business decision to sell the winery. On the other hand, if the Sisters had experienced first-hand the natural beauty of the land, and the privacy of the poustinias for retreat within walking distance of the monastery, they could consider holding on to this gem."

"Good point," Charlie said.

"However," I emphasized, "they don't want to market to the nuns when they have some guy on the lake in a raft with a beer."

"He left."

"What?"

"He left yesterday just before the cookout. Told me he missed his buddies."

I cracked up laughing, telling Charlie about the bet that the Sisters had made.

"So, we need to be clear in our marketing that this is a place of solitude, not a camp ground," Charlie said.

"Exactly. And we need to get some of the nuns from the mid-west here to visit." Charlie nodded in agreement.

"I have another question. Remember when Maggie was here and her husband joined her? Are there arrangements for married couples?"

"Not really. The poustinias were designed for one person. And if I get your point about marketing to the sisters, I don't think nuns on retreat would want to share their solitude with twosomes. Besides, I know for sure that Tony doesn't want to build more cabins."

"Agreed. But is there any way a couple could stay as guests, but not in the poustinias, and not needing to build more cabins?

"Nope."

"What about the monastery?"

"You're already planning what to do with the mansion when the nuns are gone?" Charlie responded incredulously.

"No. I'm thinking out loud. That place is so big. You've done some handyman work there. How difficult would it be to put up a few walls, and create a separate wing for a bed and breakfast, with no intrusion on the privacy of the Sisters?"

Charlie gave a low whistle. "Whew, I don't know about that one, Vicki."

"Think about it, Charlie. When you walk in the front door, there's that fabulous grand staircase, and there's an elevator at the end of the hall. I'm assuming there are bedrooms and bathrooms on the second floor of that wing."

"There are, but they don't have separate bathrooms for each bedroom."

"Many B&B's don't have en-suite bathrooms. I wouldn't expect constant reservations because the monastery isn't a destination location, but I can picture that it could be a getaway for couples who don't want to rough it."

I could see that Charlie was thinking.

"Well, I guess Jake would appreciate extra business at the diner."

Charlie motioned for the waitress, and asked for a piece of cherry pie. I ordered the same.

"That's my next point," I said. "Where's everyone go to eat around here?"

Charlie looked at me as if I had two heads.

"Don't tell me you're thinking about providing food at the monastery."

"They already provide food at the monastery."

"You know what I mean."

"Why not? There's a large dining room and kitchen. Think about it, Charlie. Where do people from town go to eat?"

"Jake's Diner."

"Where do guests of the poustinias go when they want a good meal?"

"Jake's Diner."

"Where do couples go on a date?"

"Jake's Diner."

"Where do families celebrate a special occasion?"

"A back yard barbecue... OK, Jake's Diner."

"I think there's a need in this town to have options other than Jake's place, no disrespect intended," I whispered. "And let the nuns get the profit."

Charlie was deep in thought. Finally he said, "Well, since we're going all out here, why not have a little gift shop on the first level of the mansion—Tony's big office would be a good place—where we sell the nun's wine, Sister Julie's grape jellies, and maybe my birdhouses? Heck, I can think of a lot of things we could sell."

I sat back and smiled. "Now you've got my drift, Charlie."

"You're definitely on to something, but there's no way that Tony and the nuns are going to go for it. Nope, absolutely no way. I need to wrap my head around all of this."

"Quite frankly, I do too. These ideas just started to gel today. And I hadn't thought about the gift shop."

"All of it would cost a lot of money. That's not even counting whether Tony and the girls would consider giving up a wing of the mansion."

"Yep."

We sat in silence, deep in thought. Our waitress came by, and I asked for separate checks.

"I think we both need to mull, Charlie. How about if we each take a piece to work on? You know the monastery. Do you think you could sketch out a design that would close off the wing, and leave the Sisters with their own autonomy? While you're doing that, I'll work up a cost and projected revenue spreadsheet, and see if I can find any way to get financial backing. I'll need some estimates from you for construction costs.

"Got it," Charlie said.

I reached over to shake Charlie's hand. "We do make a good team."

Chapter 27

The next morning, I checked in with Myra and my office. Harvey was content, though showing signs of missing me, and my secretary said work was piling up on my desk. I assured both of them that I'd be home in just a few days. I also gave a quick call to Amanda, wishing her a great first day of classes.

I started a list of items that I'd need to research in order to create an expense and income spreadsheet. Without access to the financial reports of the monastery, I'd have to get cost information for similar enterprises from the internet when I got home.

I mulled about how to get monetary backing to support our projects. There may be grants available for non-profit organizations. A capital campaign might be an option, but I felt certain the monastery would have to initiate such an intense venture.

In the long-run, I decided our best route might be to solicit donations, and raise additional money through sales. After all, the Girl Scouts supported their organization selling cookies. I wondered if Amanda could get some of her friends to make and sell baked goods. Not a bad idea!

That evening I called Betty to get her feedback. I began by telling her of my brainstorming session with Charlie.

"I thought we decided this was none of your business," Betty replied, with an emphasis on *we*.

"I know *we* did, but I just can't seem to let it go."

"And what does Sister Tony think of this plan that you and Charlie have concocted?"

"We can't tell her yet. It has to be her idea."

"How, pray-tell, do you intend for this scheme to be Tony's idea—mental telepathy?"

"That's Charlie's department. But if anyone can do it, he can."

"Here's what I think," Betty said. "If the Sisters came to me asking for donations because they want to create a B&B, restaurant, and gift shop at the monastery, I'd support it 100%."

"Good, because that's what they're going to do."

"I think a B&B would create an opportunity for couples— or even singles who prefer a comfortable setting over rustic—to have a serene retreat," Betty said. "Of course you'd need to provide at least breakfast, but it makes sense to offer meal service which the Sisters need anyway, and the facilities are already there. Creating a small gift shop is very common at wineries, and not unheard of at monasteries open to the public. They could even sell visors, and things like that."

"Very funny. So, are you in?"

"I'm in if it's what the Sisters want."

"Are you in to help me raise the money for renovations, if that's what the Sisters want?" I badgered.

"Yes, I'm in. And, quite honestly, we should probably recruit Jeff Stodges if all of this moves forward."

"That's a great idea! I'm sure he has lots of connections, and he's already personally supported the Sisters."

I could feel my excitement taking hold of me. I guess Betty could sense my enthusiasm because she said, "Whoa, Nellie! Don't put the cart before the horse. We do no soliciting until Sister Tony initiates such a venture."

"Got it. We'll let Charlie do his magic."

^^^

The rest of the week was a whirlwind of activity. Harvest began at 7 a.m. each day, and ended when Charlie deemed the task was completed.

At one point, Charlie told me that they had investigated mechanical harvesting of the grapes, but the Sisters liked providing jobs for the migrant workers. Hand picking also reaped a better harvest with less damage to the fruit.

As usual, the Sisters provided a hearty lunch, and sent the harvesters home with their pay. Each afternoon, I sat with a different group and enjoyed the camaraderie. I learned of the challenges of moving from farm to farm, and that many of the workers sent money home to their families.

At the luncheon on the last day of the harvest, Tony and Charlie joined the group at the table I was sitting. Despite the exhaustion each of us felt, everyone was in great spirits. Tony announced that this year's harvest had the best yield in the history of the vineyard. We all cheered.

When they left, each of the farmhands got a jar of Sister Julie's grape jelly, and a bonus in their envelopes. I didn't take any money, but I was thrilled to get the jelly.

A few of the Sisters began putting the leftovers away. Tony asked Charlie to bring a few more bottles of iced tea and soda to the table.

"Let's just take a little time to unwind before we pack up the grapes," she said. Then Sister Tony turned to me. "I know you'll be leaving us tomorrow, and I'll miss you. In such a few short months, you've become part of our family. We hope you'll be back soon."

I assured Tony that I was already checking my calendar to see if I could arrange a few days in October.

"That would be wonderful. Next month is apple-picking time around here, and those of us who can, help one of our neighbors who has an orchard. To be honest, the Sisters just collect the apples that have fallen to the ground, but we have a lot of fun."

"In fact," Tony continued, "I was thinking that we should have a Thanksgiving celebration this year. It might be our last Thanksgiving at the monastery, and I'd like to invite our dearest friends to join us."

Charlie agreed that was a great idea, and I told them that I'd definitely come.

"When you talk to Betty and Amanda, tell them to save the date," Tony said. "We'll also invite Amanda's dad, as well as Jeff Stodges and his wife, and Maggie and her husband. I'll send out invitations next month."

"Have you heard any more about the possible merger of the Sisters?" I asked.

"I feel certain that it will happen sooner or later. As our numbers dwindle, it's the best way to preserve our history. Joining forces can be very beneficial. I'd just like to preserve the Monastery of St. Carmella. The Sisters in the mid-west branch aren't really aware of what we have here. Of course, they know that the land and the vineyards are valuable, but I'd hate to see them sell it."

"Is there any possibility that there could be a merger and still keep this place as a community asset?"

"I'm working on that. Charlie and I were chatting about it just the other day. I've decided to create a brochure that would advertise the poustinias as a retreat for our Sisters in the mid-west. If fact, I've already received permission to hand-deliver the brochures to their Motherhouse in St. Louis, and meet with the Sisters in administration."

I swear Charlie winked at me.

"And now that I think about it," Tony continued, "I'm going to also invite them here for Thanksgiving. They can see firsthand what a gem we have, and they'd be able to meet you and the others who have been such a support."

Charlie lifted his soda and said, "Cheers!"

I followed suite, and agreed it was a great plan. Tony looked like a heavy burden had been lifted from her shoulders.

Chapter 28

Before I left on Saturday, Charlie brought over a simple sketch of renovations that would be needed if we moved forward with the next step of our plan. I couldn't imagine when he found the time this week to work on the project, but I recognized that he was as excited as I about the potential for new revenue.

He showed me that a wall could be constructed on both floors to close off the west wing of the Monastery. The main front door would be the entrance for the B&B and restaurant, with the gift shop on the first floor.

Although the Sisters had a back door off the screened porch, and a side door off the east wing, he suggested that the side door be converted to a more stately entrance to their residence. A new elevator and a small kitchen would need to be installed, and one of the unused offices on the first floor could be converted to a small dining room for the Sisters.

Charlie suggested painting the second floor for the B&B, and providing more appropriate décor in the bedrooms. He added that we should also plan for the expertise of an architect.

We reviewed my list of expenses and added items that I hadn't included.

"We're going to need more money than I originally anticipated," I told Charlie.

He agreed and said, "Do you have any ideas for potential donors? Jeff Stodges may be willing to help."

I told Charlie of my conversation with Betty, and that we planned to contact Jeff if the Sisters approved the renovations. Charlie disagreed.

"Tony won't begin to come up with this idea if she doesn't know that financial backing is available."

"I understand. Let me see what I can do to get us started."

I explained that I was going to ask Amanda and her friends to run some bake sales, and I could also get my firm to contribute to the monastery.

"Good idea," Charlie said. "I can make some birdhouses to sell. I also might be able to get the guys at the Fire House to sponsor extra Bingo games to benefit the Sisters. Maybe they'll let me purchase some boxes of pull-tabs to sell at the games. They're the big money-maker."

^^^

When I arrived home, I fetched Harvey as soon as I unloaded the car. Myra had seen me pull into the driveway, and had packed all of his belongings. We sat on her front porch, and I told her about the grape harvest, and my canoe skills, and even my swim in the cold lake.

"I can see that this place in the woods has been good for you. You seem to have a new expression and a sparkle in your eyes."

Harvey was nudging me, and I reached down to pet him.

"I don't know what's happening in me, Myra. I feel more alive than I have in years."

I put Harvey on the leash and gathered his bag. As he pulled me down the steps, I turned and said, "By the way, I'd like you to call me Vicki."

Myra gave me a look with raised eyebrows.

"What's that all about? Next thing I know, you'll be moving to a shack in the woods, and growing all of your own fruits and vegetables."

"I doubt it," I chuckled. I reminded her of Amanda's makeover scheme. "I think the name Vicki is much less formal. Besides, I promised Amanda that I'd loosen up."

Myra laughed and shook her head.

"Well, Miss Vicki. You're definitely getting loosen-er. Amanda will be impressed!"

^^^

The week was a whirlwind of activity between catching up at work and home. In the evenings I did internet searches to cost out things that we'd need to create the B&B at the monastery. When I found a comparable and reasonable estimate, I added it to my spreadsheet. The final tally indicated that we'd need a fairly substantial sum of money to begin renovations, but the estimated revenue when they were finished could balance the budget within a relatively short time.

On Wednesday evening, I called Amanda to see how she was feeling, and to ask how her classes were progressing. She said she was doing well, but she couldn't talk long because she and Kate were going to the library to do research for a class assignment.

Amanda and I made plans to have lunch on Saturday, as she was eager to show me her new apartment. I reminded myself to stop at the florist so I could pick out a plant for a housewarming gift.

I selected the most colorful outfit I had in the closet on Saturday morning, and donned my largest and gaudiest dangling earrings. Using the GPS, I had no trouble finding her place. She and Kate have a second floor apartment with a cute little balcony. I could see that my pretty peace lily would make a nice addition.

When I texted her that I had arrived, Amanda came out to show me where to park. She laughed when she noticed my fashion statement. I'm not sure whether that meant she liked it, or if she thought it was awful.

Kate and Amanda excitedly showed me their little place. They each have a nice size bedroom, and they share the hall bathroom. Though the living room is small with mismatched furnishings, it's cozy and inviting. Large sliding glass doors open to the balcony. The kitchen has white cabinets with a large breakfast counter, and a corner nook with a bistro table and two chairs. Amanda's bedroom is off the living room, and Kate's bedroom is down the hall.

Kate joined us for lunch, and the girls exuberantly told me about their first week of classes, their classmates, and the socials they had attended. They explained that there were 12 students in their cohort-based program, which meant that they all started at the same time, and they were all taking the same courses. They seemed to like the fact that there were eight guys to four girls, upping their chances for dating opportunities.

Their introductory food prep course focused on knife skills and *Mise en Place*, which Amanda explained was making sure you had everything you needed at your cooking station before you got started. Neither of the girls was crazy about the culinary math course, but agreed it would be helpful in recipe conversions. Their favorite course was called Baking and Sweet Treats, where they would learn the fundamentals of making cakes, pies, cookies, and candy.

That was a perfect segue for me to ask the girls if they would be able to host some bake sales to raise money to donate to the Sisters at the monastery. They thought it would be a fabulous way to hone their baking skills and provide community service, both of which were recommended in their program. They weren't sure if they'd be allowed to sell their goods on campus, but promised to check it out on Monday.

Kate and Amanda began to excitedly discuss who they could recruit to join them, what they could make, and how they should price each item. I chuckled to myself, thinking they'd also be getting practice with their culinary math skills. I gave them $100 as seed money to purchase ingredients.

It was late afternoon when we said our farewells. I knew the girls planned to go to the movies that night with a few of their classmates, and I wanted to get home before dark. I was pleased that Amanda and Kate were adjusting so well to their new routines, and happy that they were going to do the bake sales. Now I had to figure out what I was going to do to raise money.

Chapter 29

B etty and I chatted by phone each week. It amazed me that our conversations never seemed to lull. Our exchanges seemed to energize each of us.

We decided to plan a long weekend at the poustinias in October. I reminded Betty that we'd be getting an invitation to Thanksgiving dinner at the monastery. During one of our discussions, I shared that Myra and I were organizing a yard sale to raise money for the Sisters. I'd been going through boxes in the garage, tagging unused items that might sell.

"I thought we weren't going to solicit funding until the Sisters decided they wanted a B&B," Betty said.

"Charlie told me that Tony would never consider such extensive renovations without knowing that she had some financial backing. We figure that we could all raise money for the Sisters, and they can use it in whatever way they see fit."

"I guess that makes sense. I'll see if I can get donations from some of my lawyer friends. Maybe some of my teens could sell candy bars or something."

"That'd be great. Amanda and Kate are going to have some bake sales. Even though we need to generate a substantial amount of money, every little bit helps."

Before hanging up, we decided to check our calendars for the Columbus Day weekend, and make our reservations for the poustinias. I was looking forward to seeing Betty, Charlie, and the Sisters again.

^^^

Amanda and I touch base often. By the end of September, she and Kate had organized three bake sales that they had been given permission to host at the college's campus center. With the help of their culinary friends, they had already made almost $200. They were planning another in early October.

Amanda mentioned that she had to buy some pants with an elastic waistband. We both laughed, and I could only imagine her chagrin of wearing older lady attire.

"The exciting part," she said, "is that I can now feel the baby moving."

"That's wonderful! How are you feeling?"

"I'm great. I seem to need a little more sleep than usual, but I go to bed early—except when I go out with Joe."

"Joe? Who's Joe?"

Amanda cracked up laughing. "Don't worry, Victoria, he's just one of the guys in my cohort."

"By the way," I said. "You can call me Vicki."

"Wow, you really are loosening up. First those ridiculous earrings, and now a name change? That's awesome!"

"All right, that's enough. Tell me about Joe."

"He's really nice. We have a lot in common, and we're becoming friends. It's amazing, but his birthday is just two days before mine."

"So, he's the same age as you?"

"No, he's a year older, but it took him longer to figure out what to do with his life. He kind of got in with a bad crowd in high school, just like I did. Some of the guys he hung out with broke into a liquor store one night, and he almost got busted. The cops saw that he didn't go in, and the judge gave him a warning. She made him do community service at a homeless shelter where he worked in the kitchen. He told me that he realized one day that's where he was headed if he didn't get his act together."

"Why'd he hang around with street punks?"

"Why does anyone choose the friends they have?" Amanda retorted.

"Well, I guess I select friends who share my values, and whose company I enjoy. I just don't understand why a nice guy would associate with people who would commit robbery. My grandmother used to say, 'If you lie, you steal; if you steal, you cheat; and if you cheat, you're no good.'"

"Joe doesn't lie, steel, or cheat. He didn't have the role models you apparently had."

"Where were his parents?"

"Joe's parents split up when he was a little kid. His dad disappeared, and his mom was a heavy drinker who could barely hold down a job long enough for them to stay in one place. He was put in foster care until his mother got her act together, then she'd fall off the wagon again. But he stuck by her all those years, which is more than you could say for his dad."

"I see your point. So, do you think Joe's friends validated him, and that's why he liked their company?"

"I think Joe thought he wasn't worthy of better friends. That's what happened to me after my mom died. My dad went into his shell, and didn't even seem to notice whether I was home or not."

"Do you think you were trying to get his attention?"

"I never thought about it that way. I just know that my friends accepted me for who I was. I didn't have to put on airs or pretend to be me."

"Do you still consider your old crowd to be your friends?"

"Are you kidding? They betrayed me. Besides, I'm different now."

"You're still the beautiful young woman with the outgoing personality you were then. You just began to recognize that you have worth, that you have talents, that you deserve better, and that your dad really does love you." Amanda laughed.

"I'm not so sure about all of that, but I do like my new friends," Amanda said. "They're pretty awesome."

"It seems to me that Joe was lucky the Judge went easy on him," I said.

"When you meet him, you'll see what a good guy he is. In fact, he's one of the best helpers at our bake sales. He makes the most amazing cupcakes!"

I told Amanda that I was looking forward to meeting Joe. We made plans for me to visit the following Saturday, and I'd help with their next bake sale. In fact, I promised to make some brownies and some cookies. Maybe I could get Myra to make a few pies for the cause. Amanda said she'd be sure that Joe was there.

Chapter 30

Amanda, Joe, and Kate met me at their apartment parking lot and, after transferring my bake sale contributions, we drove to their school together in Kate's car. They had already loaded the trunk with their numerous goodies so that we could set up the bake sale before the lunch crowd got to the campus center.

Joe seemed a little nervous to meet me, but the lively chatter and bantering among us helped alleviate his apprehension. Joe's a nice looking boy, with blond hair, blue eyes, and freckles. A good foot taller than Amanda, Joe epitomizes his Irish heritage, and Amanda can't deny her Italian ancestry. They make a striking couple.

Once we arrived at our destination, Joe orchestrated the bake sale set-up. The girls and I arranged the table décor with price cards, while Joe and some of his buddies unloaded the car. Other culinary classmates were adding their own yummy-looking concoctions to join ours. Before long, a throng of students surrounded the tables, eager to purchase snacks for the day.

I could see that the culinary artists knew their roles, and the sale was progressing nicely. I stepped back and watched how well the group worked together. As the crowd thinned and the baked goods disappeared, the selling crew re-organized the display until every item was sold. Luckily, I had bought four of Joe's famous cupcakes to bring to Myra, and they were tucked away in the trunk of Kate's car. At least I hoped they were.

After we cleaned up our area of the campus center, Amanda suggested that we get some lunch in the cafeteria, and then do a campus tour. College cafeterias are not what they were in my day. I was amazed at the inviting arrangement and selection of foods at various stations throughout the dining room. There was a huge salad bar in the center of the room. Along the side walls were a pizza bistro, a sandwich deli, an ice cream parlor, and a dessert cart. The entire back of the room by the kitchen had several steam tables with brunch items, as well as lunch entrees. I had a difficult time deciding which station to visit.

In the end, I selected the deli, and had a Reuben with a side salad. Amanda chose French toast and bacon from the brunch table, Joe got chicken nuggets with cheese fries, and Kate ordered a Calzone from the pizzeria. We joined up at a table for four near the massive windows overlooking the campus.

Amanda pointed out the library, the gym, the center for liberal studies, and the science building. The culinary program is in the nutrition building around the corner. I was surprised to see so many students milling about campus on a Saturday, but realized that the school is an inviting mecca of activities.

"So, tell me, Joe," I said. "What got you interested in a culinary career?" I could see Amanda rolling her eyes.

Without hesitation, Joe said, "Last year I worked in a soup kitchen for the homeless. I worked my way up from washing pots and pans, to prepping vegetables. Eventually, I got a chance to be a line cook. That was really awesome."

Amanda appeared to relax a little when she saw how comfortable Joe seemed to be.

"A line cook has to be a really stressful job. Why'd you like it so much?" I asked.

"I guess it's because I discovered that I can make cool stuff that looks and tastes good. Our guests—that's what we called the people who came to the soup kitchen—really praised my cooking. We didn't make just soup, although we always had a fresh pot going. We cooked real food, like a hearty meal. I liked trying new recipes, and I always got compliments. That was kind of new to me."

Amanda smiled and gave Joe encouragement with her eyes. "Tell Vicki what your boss did for you."

"I was really lucky. The director of the soup kitchen is a priest. He called me into his office one day, and I was pretty nervous that I was in trouble or something. Instead, he told me that the guests really liked my food, and he wondered if I wanted to go to culinary school. I told him that I didn't have any money to pay for an education, but I'd work hard to learn what I could from the other cooks. Before you know it, he starts telling me that his foundation wanted to offer me a full scholarship."

"Wow, that's fabulous!"

"I know. I couldn't believe it! Nothing like that ever happened to me before."

"He must have seen that you have talent, and that you'll work hard to make him and his foundation proud."

"You're not kidding. I told him I'd pay him back some day, but he told me he just wants me to pay it forward. It's one of the reasons I want to help with the bake sales for the nuns."

I could see why Amanda liked this young man. Joe's a good guy who had been trapped in a lousy situation growing up. A botched robbery, a wise judge, a soup kitchen, and an understanding priest have given him the strength to find his way in life.

"OK, enough about Joe," Amanda said. "I want to show you around campus, and take you to the culinary kitchens. You're going to be so impressed!"

We gathered our trays, brought them to the washing station, and began our tour. By the time we got to their building, I was grateful that the classrooms were locked, and I wouldn't have to go through each one. Still, Amanda had me look through the windows on the doors, and I had to give the appropriate responses to the highlights of each room. I was ecstatic that Kate offered to go get her car from the parking lot at the campus center, and pick us up in front of the nutrition building.

The sun was waning by the time we arrived at the girls' apartment. The trio of friends told me that they were going to the movies, and I was welcome to join them, but I begged off. I needed to get home to feed Harvey and rest my weary bones. Amanda reached into her pocket and handed me a huge wad of bills.

"I don't know how much is there," she said, "but I think we did pretty well for the nuns today."

"You guys are awesome! Thank you."

Amanda threaded her arms with Joe and Kate. "We *are* pretty awesome," she said as I got into my car. "And you're not bad yourself!"

Chapter 31

Betty and I were both able to get poustinia reservations for the Columbus Day weekend in October, as well as the Thanksgiving weekend in November. Thank goodness Myra was so accommodating to agree to dog-sitting.

"I like the company," she said, referring to Harvey, "and I'm not going anywhere. In fact, I'm hosting Thanksgiving this year with Kate's family, so he'll enjoy the festivities. The best part is that I don't have to do a thing. Kate's cooking, and I get to just sit and look pretty."

The foliage in October was beautiful as I journeyed to the monastery. A cacophony of vibrant reds, oranges, yellows, and still some greens played with the late Friday afternoon sun. I was looking forward to seeing Betty, the Sisters, and Charlie, and having three days to re-energize.

When I arrived, Tony was helping Betty put her things in the golf cart. We loaded my bags and hopped in. Tony took us the scenic route, and the three of us were chit-chatting about what we all had been doing the past month.

I told the girls about my recent visit with Amanda, and meeting her new friend, Joe Henderson. Tony seemed surprised that Amanda was dating, but I reassured her that Joe seemed to be a nice young man, and they had similar interests.

"What's he look like?"

"He looks as Irish as they come. He's average height, nice build, blond hair, freckles, and sparkling blue eyes. The tattoos down his arms are impressive."

"Oh, Lordy," Tony gasped, and Betty laughed.

"What really intrigued me is the connection I saw between the two of them. They're in the same classes at school, they both like to cook, and they invent these quirky little competitions between each other."

"Does this boy know that Amanda's pregnant?"

"I don't know. She's so petite that she's barely showing yet. He might, though, because he seemed attentive that she didn't do any heavy lifting."

Uh-oh. I'd better be careful. I didn't want Tony to know that I was helping them set up the bake sale.

"What kind of heavy lifting would she be doing?"

"We went shopping, and Joe carried all of the bags."

Once again, I lied to a nun.

Tony pulled up to Betty's poustinia, and we unloaded her bags on the front porch. Betty promised to come over to my cabin shortly, as I had enticed her with the rotisserie chicken I had brought. On the way to my cabin, Tony mentioned that Jeff Stodges would also be a guest for the weekend.

"Too bad his wife can't join him."

Tony looked at me strangely.

"It's funny you would say that. Charlie said the exact same thing to me last week when I gave him the guest list."

"Betty told me that Jeff's wife wouldn't enjoy a weekend in the woods. Besides, the poustinias were built for just one person."

"It *is* too bad," Tony agreed. "However, I want to keep the cabins as a private place of solitude."

She helped me put my bags on the porch.

"We have plenty of room in the big mansion, but the Sisters would certainly be opposed to having paying guests intruding on their solitude."

"You might be surprised. It could be an option."

Tony chuckled and said, "My mind never stops thinking of ways we can keep this place going."

"By the way," I said. "I'd really like it if you'd call me Vicki."

"If I didn't know better," Tony mused as she released the parking break, "I'd think there was something going on between you and Charlie. That's what he calls you."

∧∧∧

There was a crisp chill in the air the next morning, but the day was bright and sunny. Betty and I planned to meet in the parking lot at 10 a.m. to go to Jake's Diner for breakfast. We figured the early birds would have finished eating by then, and we'd have a better chance of finding a table for two.

The place was packed, but as I glanced around the room, I noticed Charlie and Jeff seated at a booth by the windows. I nudged Betty to follow me. Charlie waved when he saw us, and motioned for us to join them.

The waitress brought over two more place settings and menus, and told us she'd give us a few minutes to make our selections. Charlie had a big stack of pancakes with bacon on the side, and Jeff had a western omelet. I realized I had never actually met Jeff, so I introduced myself.

"Hi, I'm Vicki."

Betty choked on her water. I guess I forgot to tell her about the Vicki thing.

"Nice to meet you, Vicki. I'm Jeff."

Betty was right. Jeff is very good-looking.

"Charlie was just beginning to tell me about the plan you two have concocted," Jeff said. "I understand that this has to be Sister Tony's idea. Have you made any progress on that front?"

Charlie replied that he'd been dropping hints for the last few weeks, and I mentioned that I planted a seed yesterday.

"In the meantime," I said, "we decided that we should try to raise some money for the Sisters in case they might have a use for it."

Betty signaled to the waitress that we were ready to place our orders.

Charlie told us that he had $961 from Bingo games, and I had $836 from the bake sales and yard sale. Betty added that she had another $520 from donations and candy sales. Charlie noted that he had opened a checking account at the local bank, and on Tuesday he'd deposit the money that we had brought.

"That's a good start," Jeff commented, "but not nearly enough to cover the cost of such a grand scheme. My company can contribute a substantial donation, and I have some colleagues who may be interested in helping."

We all agreed to continue our efforts. I knew my firm would give to the monastery, but I wanted to request a larger amount when I had more specific details.

Jeff and Charlie got another cup of coffee while Betty and I finished our breakfasts. We chatted more about the potential for revenue for the Sisters, and Jeff really liked the idea of the B&B.

"My wife, Kim, would honestly like the place. I can picture us enjoying a glass of wine in a comfortable room. Heck, I can see her inviting her friends and their spouses for a monastery weekend. The guys and I can fish on the lake, and they can go to the outlet mall that Tony's always talking about." We all laughed.

"On another note," I said to Charlie," when's the apple picking time at the neighboring orchard?"

Jeff and Betty looked at each other; Betty rolled her eyes.

"They're planning to start on Monday, even though it's a holiday. The Holtz's have a family-run business, so they'll get all their kids and grandkids over to harvest in the morning, then they'll have an afternoon picnic. I usually man the grill, and could use some backup if you can stay, Jeff."

"What about Betty and me?"

"Well, I just figured you'd be working with the ladies. They start peeling and coring some of the first batch to make applesauce in a big cauldron on the fire pit. It sure is tasty, too. By the way, the nuns are cooking a pot roast for dinner tomorrow. Tony told me to invite all of you. I think she wants to get us together to give her some ideas for the big Thanksgiving celebration."

"That would be enjoyable," Betty replied. "It looks like our weekend is all planned out."

"Not entirely. I thought you might all want to come to the Fire House for Bingo tonight."

"Don't you call Bingo on Friday nights?" I teased.

"I do, but this evening benefits the nuns."

Chapter 32

The next morning, I wrapped myself in the big comforter and sat on the porch with my tea. The dew glistened on the grass, and there was a light mist in the trees as the sun warmed their branches.

I reflected on the previous evening, and the bond of friendship that was developing among the poustinia dwellers. Charlie had assigned Jeff, Betty, and me to selling pull-tabs at Bingo, and we went from table to table, encouraging the players to try their luck for a good cause.

Afterwards, we stopped at Jake's place and got hot chocolate. It was close to midnight by the time we trudged from the parking lot to our cabins, laughing and chatting the entire time. The men made sure that Betty and I were safely inside our poustinias before continuing their trek through the woods.

Startled from my reverie, Charlie called out a hello, and I beckoned him to join me. He was wearing jeans and a sweatshirt, layered with a fall jacket. His cheeks were rosy, so I figured he'd been out walking, or guarding the perimeter.

"You're up and about quite early," I said.

I invited him to sit on the rocking chair next to mine.

"I love this time of year," Charlie said. "Heck, I like every season, each for its own reason. Listen to that! I made another rhyme!" We both laughed.

"Do you ever get lonely here?"

"Sometimes. I'm not really sure it's loneliness, because I have a lot of things to occupy my time. I'm pretty comfortable with myself. You know what I mean?"

"Yeah. I do."

"You know, for years I tried to run from everyone and everything. Only problem was, I couldn't run from me. My anger and my grief took over my life. Best thing I ever did was come looking for Stella's sister. Maybe Stella drew me here, knowing that I needed Tony's touch. This place has been good for me."

"I've known you only a short while, Charlie, but I've noticed some significant changes in you since we first met. You get a quirky twinkle in your eye, you laugh more readily, and you have enthusiasm in your voice."

"I can feel it, Vicki. It's like I'm coming out of darkness. You've changed too, you know. You used to be kind of stuffy."

"I was not!"

"You were," he teased. He changed the tone of his voice to a high pitched British accent. "My name is Victoria, and I'm a business executive."

"I think Amanda changed me. She taught me to be more carefree, to enjoy life. And I think this place has changed me."

Charlie reached over and put his hand on top of mine.

"You know what I think? I think we're both lucky to have been drawn to the Monastery of St. Carmella. I think we kind of found each other." I nodded in agreement.

We sat there for a while, both reflecting on this new dimension of our friendship. I knew my attraction to Charlie had been growing and evolving, but the reality of the moment caught me by surprise. I thought any possibility of love had escaped me, yet it found me when I no longer sought it.

"I'm a little set in my ways," I said. Charlie laughed and said, "I am too."

"I need to take things slowly."

Charlie agreed. "We'll just take it one day at a time. In the meantime, come on over to my place. I want to show you the Fire House birdhouse and some new creations."

"Let me get my jacket. It's a little chilly out here this morning."

"I'll warm you up with my special brew of hazelnut coffee."

"I'm not much of a coffee drinker, but I can bring a tea bag with me."

"You can bring your tea bag, but you can't have it until you taste my specialty. I promise you'll be converted."

As we trekked through the woods, Charlie told me about the things he'd been doing during the past month. After finishing the fall clean-up of all the flower gardens, he designed a new birdhouse that he could make in just one day.

"It's a simple little construction," he said, "but I can get $15 for it. It's a big seller at Flossie's Floral Shop."

"That's great, Charlie."

"The money from that birdhouse goes directly to the nuns' fund. I didn't want to tell everyone yesterday, but I've deposited another $400 just from birdhouses."

"Why didn't you want to share that information?" I asked as we stepped onto Charlie's porch.

He opened the door and said, "I don't know. Guess I figured it'd be like tooting my own horn."

"If you want, I'll toot it for you. The others should know how much you've been doing to help the cause."

Charlie invited me to take off my jacket and sit on the stool in the kitchenette while he made a fresh pot of his brew. In just a few minutes, he had two steaming mugs, and put a big dollop of Reddi Whip on the top of each.

"I don't mind if you want to tell everyone when the time is right," he said as he moved a mug in front of me on the counter. "It'll probably come up in conversation one of these days."

The hazelnut aroma awoke all of my senses.

"Wow! This smells good, Charlie."

"It'll make a believer out of you," he chuckled.

"We'll see about that. Now show me what you've made."

The finished Fire House birdhouse was displayed in the corner of his work table, and was surrounded by a couple of completed smaller birdhouses. He had an assembly line of parts spread out on the table for the new ones he was making.

"This is so wonderful," I said as I sipped my coffee.

"What? The coffee or my work?"

"I have to admit that I do like your brew. It must be the hazelnut aroma and the whipped cream. But I love seeing what you've created in your little poustinia workshop! When are you going to present the Fire House birdhouse?"

"I was thinking maybe on Friday night when I call Bingo. The captain plans to be there this week with his wife. Some of the guys will also be there working the crowd. I think it'll be a big hit."

"It'll be a wonderful surprise for everyone. I wish I could be there for the unveiling."

"I wish you could be there, too. Can't you stay until Friday?"

"Not this time, Charlie. I have a couple of important meetings this week when I get back. Maybe you can call me and tell me about it."

"I don't have a cell phone."

"That's OK. Have someone take pictures and you can show me when I return at Thanksgiving."

"It won't be the same, but I guess that would work."

"I should get going," I said. "I'll let you have some time to work on your projects."

I placed my mug in the sink and put on my jacket,

"You can make your brew for me anytime. I really enjoyed it."

Charlie opened the door for me.

"I knew you would. I'll catch up with you at the monastery about 4 p.m."

As I stepped off the porch, Charlie added, "By the way, we made over $1200 for the nuns last night!"

Chapter 33

I was closing my cabin door when Betty and Jeff called from the path to see if I was ready. I was glad all three of us would be arriving at the nuns' residence together. I mentioned that we should imagine ourselves in fancy attire walking through the portico to the new Monastery Restaurant. Betty chuckled but said that the name didn't grab her.

"How about the Country Squire?" Jeff suggested.

"That's got a ring to it," Betty replied, "but isn't a squire a gentleman? It doesn't seem right to name the place after a guy."

We were all laughing when Charlie opened the door, and took our jackets. I whispered to him that we were picking out names for the restaurant.

Charlie led us to the community room where the Sisters were gathering. Tony invited us to make ourselves comfortable, and asked Jeff to pour the wine. Charlie began taking around a tray of hors d'oeuvres, when Julie and Dolores arrived with more tasty tidbits. I took a sip of the pinot noir and commented on its vividly fruity taste. Tony noted that it was one of their most popular wines, although it had taken years to perfect the recipe.

Dolores returned to announce that we should make our way to the dining room. We gathered around the long table, with Sister Tony at the head. Charlie sat to my left, while Betty and Jeff sat across from us. The other Sisters filled in, and I counted 11 of us. Platters of food were placed strategically down the center of the table.

The Sisters bowed their heads while Tony said the blessing. After a chorus of "Amen," Tony raised her glass of wine and proposed a toast to friendship. We clinked our glasses and took a sip of our wine.

As if that were the signal, Julie and Dolores started passing the platters of food family-style. In addition to the pot roast and gravy, there was a medley of carrots, parsnips, and roasted potatoes, and a green bean casserole. The conversation was as hearty as our appetites.

When dessert was served, Tony announced that she would like some input to prepare for Thanksgiving.

"I received word yesterday that four of the Sisters from the mid-west province will be joining us. Two of them will be arriving at the beginning of the week, and would like to stay in the poustinias." Charlie turned to smile at me.

"The other two Sisters will arrive on Wednesday afternoon, and I'll meet them at the airport. They'll stay in the monastery. Dolores, could you make sure the guest rooms are ready? Unfortunately, Maggie and her husband won't be able to join us. Maggie just learned that she's expecting, and she's been experiencing a lot of morning sickness."

"That's great news! Not so much about the morning sickness," I said, "but I'm so happy that she's going to be a mother. The miracle of the poustinias!"

"Now, Jeff..." Tony started.

"Kim and I'll be coming in time for Thanksgiving dinner. We'll head home after the festivities."

Julie said, "That's crazy! We have plenty of room here. In fact, there's a whole unused wing with six bedrooms and three baths on the second floor. Dolores and I were just saying the other day that it's a shame we can't make better use of that space. Don't you think we could invite Jeff and his wife to stay with us Thanksgiving night?"

Charlie nudged my arm. Tony looked at the smiling faces of the nuns. They were all echoing their approval.

"What do you think, Jeff?" Tony asked.

"Gosh, I honestly think Kim would enjoy staying, and I'd certainly like not to have a late night drive home. Of course, we'd pay for our room."

"Most certainly not!"

"Why not?" I interrupted. "Betty and I'll be paying for our weekend in the poustinias."

"That's a good point," Tony said. "No one will be paying to stay."

There was a cacophony of voices around the table.

"No, that's not what I was trying to say," I said. "We'll be your guests for Thanksgiving dinner, but we want to pay for our overnight accommodations. We don't want to intrude on your personal space. Jeff and Kim can stay in the separate wing and use the main staircase. They won't need any access to the main part of the mansion."

"Exactly," Jeff said. "Think of us as overnight patrons. It's the only way we'll agree to stay."

"I'm not sure what we'll do," Tony replied. "I also invited Amanda and her father. I can't very well tell them they'll have to pay."

"I can," I said. "Julie said there's plenty of room in that wing. Amanda can have her own room, her dad another, and if you tell Amanda she can bring her friend Joe, there's even a room for him. I'll pay for Amanda's room."

"And I'll pay for Joe's room," Betty said.

"Her dad can pay for his own room," Jeff said, "And I'll chaperone." We all laughed.

"You know, Tony," one of the older Sisters from the end of the table said, "we could put some life back into this place, and make some money doing it!"

Charlie looked at me and winked. Tony looked flabbergasted, especially as the Sisters started high-fiving each other. I realized at that moment that Charlie had been weaving his magic craft with the old girls.

"Obviously, if we have overnight guests at the mansion," Dolores said, "we'll need to provide some breakfast the next morning. I volunteer to whip up something that everyone would enjoy."

Four other Sisters offered to help. Jeff suggested to add the cost of the meal into the fee for accommodations.

"Good idea," Betty noted. "Could you cost out how much you would charge if guests of the poustinias wanted to have breakfast at the monastery?"

"Dear God in heaven! We're not going to become a boarding house!"

"Of course not," Julie replied. "My nephew told me that he and his wife like to visit bed and breakfasts all over the place. They called them B&B's, and they like them better than motels."

"My wife and I like them, too," Jeff said. "Each one is unique and homey. They're reasonably priced, and are more comfortable than the big box motels."

"It's certainly a good plan for Thanksgiving weekend, Tony," I said, "but would you ever consider it as a revenue stream for the monastery?"

"For darn sure!" came a voice from the end of the table. "We could knock the socks off those girls from the mid-west."

"I don't know," Sister Tony replied. "It's enticing to think that people might actually want to stay at the monastery, but I can't compromise the solitude of the Sisters. What do you think, Charlie?"

"I think it's a good idea. You have a wing that could easily be separated from the nuns' living quarters. It wouldn't take much to get permits from the town to renovate."

I could see that all of the Sisters respected Charlie's opinion.

"I have a lot to think about," Tony said. "In the meantime, the Sisters and I will reflect on your suggestions. We're happy that you'll be joining us for the Thanksgiving weekend. Tomorrow, we'll be going to Holz's orchard for some apple-picking."

We agreed to meet at 10 a.m. in the parking lot.

Charlie gathered our jackets and, though Betty and I offered to assist with cleanup, the Sisters turned us down. As the four of us headed to our cabins, I pushed Charlie and said, "You've been working on the old girls, you weasel!"

"I didn't know if it would work, but I guess it did. Tony'll mull through to Thanksgiving. I know her like the back of my hand!"

"You did well," Betty added. "And you did, too, Jeff."

"If we had staged it, it couldn't have gone better." I said. "Now it's in the hands of the nuns."

^^^

I had all sorts of weird dreams last night. In one segment, crowds were thronging to the B&B. In another, I was welcoming visitors to the poustinias. I tried to recapture some of the images, but memories of the dreams soon faded as I showered and dressed for apple harvesting.

When we arrived at the Holtz's place, Jeff and Charlie joined the guys. They were each given a ladder, and reminded how to use their snipping tools on the ripe apples high in the trees. Betty and I, with the nuns and grandchildren, basketed the apples that fell to the ground. Soon we had enough fruit to begin preparing the cauldron for apple sauce.

After the women peeled and cored the ripe fruit, Mrs. Holtz added sugar, cinnamon, and her special blend of spices to create an aromatic concoction. The kids soon tired of their tasks. I could see that they were having more fun chasing each other around the yard. Sister Julie caught their attention, and enticed them to join her for a story time.

Eventually, Charlie fired up the grill. He and Jeff began cooking the chicken, hamburgers, and hot dogs. Mrs. Holtz and her daughters began bringing out the potato salad, rolls, and condiments. We enjoyed our picnic lunch around the camp fire, basking in its warmth on a crisp fall day. It was a delight to watch the grandchildren make their s'mores with graham crackers, roasted marshmallows, and melted chocolate.

Those of us who had to leave bid our farewells, but not before having a taste of warm applesauce with a scoop of vanilla ice cream. Charlie drove Betty, Jeff, and me back to the poustinias. He helped each of us gather our bags, then brought us to the parking lot to load our cars.

Jeff was the first to go, and we waved him off, promising to see him and Kim at Thanksgiving. Then I gave Betty a hug as she prepared to leave.

"This was such an enjoyable weekend," I said. "I'm so glad we came."

"Me, too. It was fun to be a part of the apple harvest."

Charlie and I both agreed. Betty settled into the driver's seat, and we said goodbye.

"I'll call you tomorrow evening," I said as Betty pulled out of the parking lot.

Alone now, I looked into Charlie's eyes, and we held hands.

"I'll be back soon," I said.

"You'd better be." He kissed me on the forehead. "I'm looking forward to Thanksgiving!"

Chapter 34

In one of my phone conversations with Amanda, she told me that she planned to keep the baby. I reminded her that it wouldn't be easy to start the new semester with a new-born.

"I know that, Vicki, but there's no way that I could give up my little girl. I thought you'd be happy about it."

"I'm very happy that you love your baby, and that you wouldn't abandon her, but adoption isn't abandonment."

I thought about Maggie and Betty who both had wanted to have a child.

"It is to me. If I have to, I'll take a leave of absence from school and get a job. But I'm keeping my baby."

"Why do you think that finding a good home for your daughter would be abandonment?"

"I know some girls who put their babies up for adoption because they didn't want to deal with a kid. I also found an internet blog of women who chose to use adoption, and many of them had a lot of regrets. Look how many times you see on Facebook that mothers are searching for the child they bore, and kids are looking for their birth parents."

"I don't do Facebook."

"Well, you should! You'd see what I'm talking about. I know you're trying to give me advice, but you're not seeing my side of it."

"I think I can see the whole picture more clearly than you're seeing it. I can be more objective."

"I don't need objectivity. I love my baby and I'm keeping her."

I knew this wasn't the time to argue with Amanda. If I backed her into a corner, she'd resist listening to any of my suggestions. I've learned enough to know that Amanda needs space when she's faced with difficult situations.

"You know that you and the baby can stay with me until you're able to manage on your own."

"Thanks. But now that I've made my decision, I have time to figure out the next step."

I told Amanda that I trusted her instincts.

"Just know that you can call me anytime if you want to talk about it. Have you discussed your plans with Joe?"

"We talk about a lot of stuff. He respects my decision about the baby, though he wants me to think about a way I could stay in school. I'd like that, too, but my daughter comes first."

^^^

A few nights later, I was talking to Betty. We chatted about what we'd been doing recently, then I recounted my unease after my conversation with Amanda.

"I think you gave Amanda good advice. She has no clue on how to raise a baby alone, nor does she know the challenges she'll face."

"We don't either. Like who am I to tell her what's best for her?"

"Well, we're old enough to know that raising a child is hard work. Amanda's at an age when she should be able to enjoy life."

"I agree, but I'm just not sure that I should be giving Amanda advice about the baby."

"What's not to know? Amanda has no income, and she's trying to complete culinary school. How's she going to take care of a child, too?"

"I don't know what it's like to bond with an infant growing within me. I look at Charlie and see the deep remorse he had after giving up his child, even though I understand that he probably made the best decision he could due to his circumstances. I try to put myself in Amanda's shoes, and I have to say that I, too, would want to keep my baby."

"I hear you, but you gave good advice. Amanda shared her decision to keep the baby with you because she has confidence that you respect and support her. She knows that she can express her feelings with you, and you'll still be there for her. And don't think for a moment that she doesn't reflect on your suggestions."

"Well, she doesn't act like she does. But I guess you're right. Amanda ponders, just like I mull. All I have to do is give her the freedom to make her own choices."

Chapter 35

Aweek before Halloween, I received a distressful call from Amanda's father. It was a Saturday morning, and I had just put a load of clothes in the dryer.

"What a nice surprise!" I replied as I answered the phone, noticing Steve Angeli's name on caller-ID.

"Victoria, this is Steve Angeli."

I guess Amanda hadn't told him of my transformation to Vicki.

"Hi, Steve. How are you doing?"

"I'm OK. No, I'm not OK. I mean Amanda's not OK."

Steve seemed frazzled, and I felt a knot in the pit of my stomach.

"I just got a call from Kate that Amanda was admitted to St. Luke's Hospital in the city this morning. She didn't know any details yet, but Amanda asked for you and me. I'm on my way now."

"Oh, my goodness! Of course, I'll leave right away. It'll take me about an hour. I'll meet you there."

I let Harvey out the back door to do his business, while I gathered my purse and jacket. When he returned, I turned off the dryer and gave him a treat.

"You be a good boy. I'm going to go see Amanda."

Harvey wagged his tail, and settled in for a snooze.

I set the car GPS for the fastest route to St. Luke's, wondering all the way what could possibly have caused Amanda to be hospitalized. Steve was standing at the front entrance when I arrived.

"Amanda's having tests right now. I figured I'd wait for you here. It's something about the baby."

"Oh, no! I just talked to her a few days ago, and she sounded great."

"I know," Steve said as we walked toward the elevator. "I talked to her the other night, and she was fine. She's in room 324. I mean she'll be in room 324 when she gets back from the tests. I mean her room is 324, but she's at tests right now."

Steve was visibly shaken. I saw Kate and Joe in the third floor lounge as we stepped off the elevator. They, too, looked upset, but relieved that we were there. Both of them started speaking at the same time.

"Whoa!" I said. "One at a time. Kate, what happened?"

Kate explained that the three of them had been working late on a culinary project at school the night before, and they had been on their feet all day.

"We were all really tired, but Amanda was exhausted. Joe dropped us off at our place…"

"Joe?" Steve asked. "Who's Joe?"

"I'm Joe, sir. Joe Henderson. I'm in Amanda's class at school."

Steve seemed to focus on Joe's tattoos, and nodded.

"OK," Kate continued. "So Joe dropped us off, and it was like midnight or something. Amanda could barely get up the steps. She went right to bed, but I watched TV for a little while. I needed to unwind. You know what I mean? Anyway, next thing I know, Amanda came out of her room and she was crying. She said she felt like something was wrong with the baby."

"Was she in pain?"

"I asked her that, but she said no," Kate replied. "She said the baby stopped moving."

"Maybe the baby was just tired," Steve said, looking relieved.

"I know, sir," Joe said. "That's what I was thinking."

"Stop calling me sir," Steve replied in an irritated tone.

"Yes, sir, I will."

"OK, so then what happened?" I questioned Kate.

"Well, then I made a cup of decaffeinated tea, thinking it might help her relax. It was like 3 o'clock in the morning or something. I got Amanda settled on the sofa with a blanket and pillow, and we talked for a while. Eventually she fell asleep so I went to bed, but I left my door open so I could hear her if she needed anything."

"You did a good job, Kate," I said.

"Yeah, but when she woke up, the baby still wasn't moving. So, I called Joe and he thought we'd better bring her to the ER."

"That was smart, Joe. It was also good that you called Amanda's dad."

"Amanda wanted her dad here. She wanted you here, too, Vicki."

A physician came into the reception area and asked for Mr. Angeli.

"I'm Steve Angeli."

"I'm Dr. Ron O'Neill. Would you like to go somewhere more private so I can fill you in on Amanda's condition?"

"We're all together. Right here's fine."

Dr. O'Neill pulled up a chair and said, "We've completed the tests we needed to confirm that there's a problem with Amanda's pregnancy. The baby is no longer viable."

"What's that mean?" Kate gasped.

"It means the baby has died," Dr. O'Neill said. "It's called an intra-uterine fetal death. The baby's heart has stopped. Although it's relatively rare, it can happen during the last trimester. Ultrasound showed that the umbilical cord is wrapped around the baby's neck. That's not unusual at this stage of the pregnancy, *per se*, and it may not have been the cause of death. We'll perform an autopsy after the baby is born."

Steve slowly exhaled and said, "Is Amanda in any danger?"

"I recommend that we induce labor," Dr. O'Neill said. "It could take a day to a few days for her to give birth, but we'll monitor her for any physical signs of distress. If there's any problem, we'll do an immediate caesarean."

Steve nodded his approval.

Dr. O'Neill stood and said, "I'll have you sign the paperwork, Mr. Angeli. The nurses will start the IV, then you can all go in to be with Amanda."

We sat in silence as the doctor departed.

Finally Joe said, "Awww, man. Amanda's going to be really upset. She really wanted that baby."

"I know," I said softly.

I was overwhelmed with sadness for her.

^^^

Amanda was crying when the four of us entered her room. She held her dad's hand tightly as he leaned over to kiss her. His eyes were misty as he said, "I love you so much, honey." The rest of us echoed his sentiments, then gave them some time to be alone together.

When Steve joined us in the hallway, he said to Joe and Kate, "Amanda would like you to sit with her until she falls asleep."

Steve and I walked back to the reception area.

"I feel so helpless," Steve said. "I don't even know the right words to say."

"You said the perfect words. Amanda needs to know you love her unconditionally. That you're here for her."

"You know, I remember the day Amanda was born like it was yesterday. I was so excited to be a dad, and my wife made parenting seem so easy. She encouraged me to work towards tenure as a college professor, but that meant I was always wrapped up in my books and my research. Before I knew it, Amanda's mom got cancer, and I didn't know how to deal with it. I buried myself even more with my work."

"I hear you. Though I wasn't lucky enough to be a parent, I found it comforting to focus on work, rather than face emotional ties."

"Are you kidding? You jumped right in and took Amanda under your wing when she was struggling. I sent her to a monastery. What kind of dad is that?"

"I honestly don't know what possessed me to invite Amanda to my home for the summer. In fact, let me assure you, I messed up plenty of times. Parenting is darn hard! But I can tell you this. Amanda has changed my life."

"Really? How?"

I began to explain to Steve how stuck in my ways I had become. I told him about the changes I could see in myself, the more I opened my heart to Amanda. I shared stories about the good times and the bad, and how Amanda was working on my transformation.

"That's amazing," Steve said. "I was a little envious of how easy you seemed to be able to get through to Amanda, when I found her to be such a challenge."

"She's definitely a piece of work!" We both laughed. "I do have a question for you. Why didn't you have a funeral for Amanda's mom?"

"I couldn't," Steve said. "There was no way I could get through that terrible time with a bunch of people standing around her grave and telling me to be brave. Besides, I didn't have any family, and my wife never wanted Amanda to know about her dysfunctional relatives. Heck, I wouldn't even know where to find them."

"I wonder if you might consider some way to bring closure to Amanda's mother's death and her daughter's death. Perhaps think of it as a celebration of life for both of them.

^^^

Amanda's baby girl was born on Sunday, at 3:32 p.m. She weighed just under 3 pounds, and Amanda named her Addison Victoria. We buried her next to Amanda's mother, with a proper funeral in honor of both of them.

Chapter 36

Amanda stayed home from school the rest of the week after the funeral. On Halloween, I got a big trick or treat bag, filled it with all of her favorite candies, and drove to visit her. She was resting on the sofa when I arrived at her apartment. The living room was filled with balloons and floral displays, and a big plastic pumpkin on the coffee table was loaded with treats. I was relieved to see that she wasn't alone. Kate answered the door, and said that Joe was in the kitchen prepping for a test recipe that they were developing for an assignment.

I gave Amanda a hug and sat on the side chair.

"I guess you're relieved that my baby's gone," Amanda murmured.

Kate gasped and said, "How could you say that, Amanda? Vicki cried when the doctor told us the news. We all did!"

"Whatever," Amanda replied.

"I'm not relieved, Amanda. Addison's death is a painful experience you'll never forget. You're grieving, as we all are."

"You didn't want me to keep her anyway, so what do you care?"

Kate retreated to the kitchen.

"I certainly didn't want Addison to die."

"Well, she's gone, so you don't have to worry about it anymore. Besides, I don't want to talk about it."

"It sounds to me like we should talk about why you're angry with me."

"Because you're probably thinking, 'I told you so,' like I couldn't take care of her or something. But I did take care of her.

It wasn't my fault that she died. The doctor told me that her death wasn't because of anything I did or didn't do."

"First of all, not for one moment would I say 'I told you so!' I've never said that to you, nor have I ever thought it." I could feel my annoyance rising. "Second of all, you made sure that you did everything to protect and care for your baby. End of story! And thirdly, I've gone out of my way to give you love, respect, and support. I know you're grieving, but you don't lash out to those who care about you!"

"I told you, I don't want to talk about it!" Amanda stormed into her bedroom and slammed the door.

Joe and Kate joined me in the living room. Kate had tears in her eyes and said, "I'm so sorry, Vicki. This is how Amanda's been since the funeral. She barely talks to anyone and, if she does, she's mean and nasty. We thought she might like it if Joe and I worked on our assignment here, but she barely gets off the sofa, and doesn't seem to want any part of it. We don't know what to do."

Joe added, "We know that she's upset, but I thought it would raise her spirits if we kept her company. Nothing seems to work."

"I had the same idea you had—that she'd enjoy some companionship," I began. "None of us has had the horrible experience of losing a child. Maybe she needs time alone to begin the healing process. I don't mean that we'll desert her, because I know that she's especially going to need the two of you to be nearby. She'll reach out to us when she's ready. I feel certain of that."

"I was thinking that she might want to go to the counseling center at school," Kate said.

"She might. You could suggest that to her."

"Amanda can be a really private person," Joe said. "She may not want to be seen going into the counseling center. I thought maybe I could get her to meet Father Jim. Like maybe we could go out to dinner so that she could just talk to him. He has a real knack for knowing what to say when someone's hurting."

"I think that's a great idea, Joe. If she doesn't want to go out to dinner, you could invite him for dinner here." Joe and Kate nodded their agreement.

"In the meantime, I think we should all leave. Kate, could you surprise your parents with a visit this evening? If not, you're welcome to stay with me."

"No problem," Kate said. "I'll say I came to help them with the trick or treaters. They'll love it!"

"When should we come back?" Joe asked.

"Well, Kate will certainly have to be back by Sunday evening. You guys have school on Monday. Joe, I think you should wait until Amanda calls you. I have a feeling she'll be on the phone by tomorrow morning. In the meantime, you could try to get hold of Father Jim. Set up a meeting for early in the week."

"That sounds like a plan," Joe replied. "I sure hope it works."

"Me, too," I said as I gathered my purse and coat. "Keep me posted in case we have to set up plan B."

^ ^ ^

Betty must have mental telepathy because she called shortly after I arrived home. I began by telling her how grateful I had been that she had taken the time to go to the funeral service for Amanda's daughter and mother.

"That's why I called. I wanted to know how Amanda's doing."

"Not so good." I told her of the dismal visit I had earlier today.

"Maybe she needs time alone."

"I thought that she might want company, but now I think you may be right. I'm just not sure. There's no doubt that Amanda's depressed, and that can sometimes have devastating consequences. What if she does something to harm herself?"

"Did Amanda verbalize anything that might suggest that could happen?"

"No. She was mostly angry with me because I'm the one who advised her to put Addison up for adoption, although she hasn't been very nice to Kate or Joe either. The autopsy results indicated that the baby had a congenital heart defect that had gone undetected, and the doctor assured Amanda that she couldn't have prevented it."

"I believe that anger's an important step in the grieving process," Betty noted. "I'm sure it wasn't pleasant to be the recipient, but Amanda's lashing out is natural. You're strong enough to handle it, and Amanda's stable enough to weather this rough patch."

I told Betty that Joe planned to have his friend, Father Jim from the soup kitchen, meet with Amanda.

"I know him!" Betty exclaimed. "He's amazing. He has a delightful sense of humor, and he works wonders with those who need help. He devotes all of his time advocating for the poor, and gathering the resources they might need."

I shared with Betty what he had done for Joe.

"I'm not surprised. That's the kind of stuff he does. Do you know he's actually a licensed counselor?"

"No. I didn't know that. I wonder if Joe knows it."

"Probably not. It's not something that Father Jim advertises, but it's what makes him so effective at the homeless shelter. Joe's a lucky kid to have him as a mentor."

"I just hope we're on the right track with helping Amanda."

^^^

I decided I had better call Amanda's dad to let him know that we had left Amanda alone to grieve at her apartment. I told him what had transpired, and explained that I wasn't sure that we made the right decision. Steve said that he had called her each day, and he knew that this was a difficult time for her.

"Even though she doesn't see it, Amanda's very much like me when she's upset. I need to be by myself to process things. A lot of people don't understand that. Amanda will reach out when she's ready. I'll call her in a bit to see how she's doing, and I'll remind her that she can always come home until she's feeling better."

I told Steve about Father Jim and what Betty had shared with me about him. I explained that Joe was going to try to get Amanda to meet him.

"It can't hurt. Maybe Amanda will open up to him, maybe she won't. You know as well as I do that she can be resistant when she wants to be. Speaking of Joe, what do you think about him?"

"I like him, Steve. He's a nice kid, he's hard-working, and he's developed an inner strength that complements Amanda."

I told him about Joe's background and what Father Jim had done for him.

"Yeah, but did you see all those tattoos?" Steve moaned.

"That's just body décor for this generation. How different is it from all of Amanda's piercings? I really think they're good for each other, and Amanda's going to need him and Kate to help her get over what she has experienced."

Steve agreed to give Joe a chance, and promised to check in on Amanda. By the time we hung up, I decided to get an early supper and call it a night.

Chapter 37

I had a restless night worrying about Amanda, and wondering if we had done the right thing to leave her alone. It was a rather chilly and dreary day, and I preferred to lie in bed, huddled under the cozy quilt. Instead, I pushed myself to pull on jeans and a sweater, and make a cup of hot tea. I was reading the Sunday newspaper when Amanda called.

"I'm sorry. I didn't mean what I said to you yesterday."

"I know. This is a really difficult experience for you. Healing will come, but it's going to take time. You need to be able to grieve."

"I can't stop crying."

"Tears are good. They're therapeutic. In fact, it's important for you to express your emotions."

"I don't want to go to school tomorrow."

"I can't imagine that you could return to classes this week."

"Yeah, but I'm not sick."

"Honey, you gave birth this past week, and you had a funeral for Addison and your mother. No one would expect you to be returning to school so soon. When you feel able, maybe Kate and Joe could help you keep up with your studies at home so you don't fall too far behind. Just take it one day at a time."

"Joe wants to take me for a drive, and maybe visit the homeless shelter today."

"Do you feel able to do that?"

"Yeah, I guess so. I kind of want to get out of the apartment, but I don't want to have to talk to a bunch of people."

"Then I think you should go with Joe. You feel safe with Joe, and he's not going to put you into an uncomfortable position. Besides, he'll listen to you if you decide that you just want a Sunday afternoon drive, and don't want to visit the shelter."

"OK, I'll go. See, I really do listen to you."

∧∧∧

A few evenings later, Amanda called to update me on her progress. She told me that she actually had gone into the homeless shelter with Joe on Sunday, and he had shown her around the soup kitchen. The best part was that she had met Father Jim, who had been cutting up potatoes for a chowder.

"You'd really like him. He told me some funny stories about Joe, like the time he got stuck in the walk-in refrigerator, and stuff that Joe had never mentioned. Father Jim's really awesome! In fact, he's coming here for dinner tomorrow night. He made us promise that we wouldn't make anything fancy or extravagant. He'd rather just sit in the kitchen and chat. Don't you think that's cool? I mean like he's a priest and everything."

"So, what are you going to make for dinner?"

"Joe wants to make fish pouches. Priests probably like fish, don't you think? You just put a hunk of cod on a piece of aluminum foil, add seasonings, and throw on some vegetables like green beans and spinach, wrap it up, and put it in the oven for 20 minutes."

"That sounds easy and tasty."

"Yeah, well, Father Jim said he'd make us a deal. He said he'd come for a visit, if we'd volunteer at the soup kitchen next Saturday."

"How do you feel about that? Are you up to working?"

"Father Jim said I'm not allowed to do anything strenuous. Joe and Kate will cook, and I can help him organize papers in his office. He said his desk is a mess."

Father Jim sounds like a wise counselor, I thought to myself. I had no doubt that the quiet ambiance would give Amanda the opportunity to share her feelings, and begin to work through her grief.

"By the way," Amanda noted as we were ending our call, "I'm going to school tomorrow. My teachers said that I could just go to the lectures if I'm able, and then I can watch the demonstrations, or take the afternoons off. I think I'm going to stay and watch the demonstrations."

^^^

I called Amanda the following Saturday evening to see how she was feeling after her return to school and her day of volunteering at the shelter. She said that she was tired, but that her experience working with Father Jim was "awesome."

"His desk really was a mess, but we got it all cleaned up."

"It sounds like he needed your help."

"Yeah, I'd tell him what a paper was about, then he'd file it. We made a folder for invoices, so he'll have them all organized. You wouldn't believe how much it costs to run a food kitchen."

"Don't they get food donated from food banks?"

"Some of it's given, but they usually still have to buy ingredients. Father Jim has to go out and solicit donations all the time. That's why he doesn't have time to put his office in order. I told him about my work at your firm last summer, and I volunteered to be his office manager one day each week. Father Jim said he'd be honored if I'd help him. Can you believe that? Joe seemed happy that I offered because he said he's been wanting to volunteer more often. Even Kate had fun."

"Did Father Jim ask you about Addison?"

"Yeah, I cried a little. He didn't really even seem fazed by my tears. In fact, he told me about a Mexican lady named Maria who often stays at the shelter. Her husband and two little kids were killed in some crazy drive-by shooting last year. She ended up homeless and really depressed. He thinks I might be able to help her. He even got a little choked up telling me about her. I told him I didn't think I could help her, because I was a mess. And you know what he said?"

"What?"

"He said that he could see that I have more strength and courage than most people he meets. Can you believe that?"

"Yes, I can believe it. Someday I hope I can meet this Father Jim. He seems to have a great gift of helping others."

"By the way, Sister Tony called me to see how I was doing, and to say that Joe was also invited for Thanksgiving at the monastery. Joe said he'd like to see the place, but he never thought he'd be having Thanksgiving dinner with a bunch of nuns. My dad's going to pick us up on his way, and we're all going to stay overnight. Do you think it's a good idea?"

"If you're up to it, I think it's a wonderful idea."

"Yeah, but dad better not give Joe a hard time."

I assured Amanda that her dad had already seen Joe's good qualities, and he recognized the value of their friendship.

"Just don't spill the beans about the bake sales," I said, explaining that we were hoping the Sisters would decide to start a B&B. "Thanksgiving will be a trial run. At some point during the weekend we'll surprise the Sisters with the money we've raised."

"Cool! I'll tell Joe to keep his mouth shut. We were happy to add a couple of hundred bucks to the pot."

Before we disconnected, we agreed that she could show Joe and her dad the poustinia I was staying in when they arrived, then we could all walk together to Thanksgiving dinner at the monastery.

Chapter 38

The forecasters projected that we might have an early winter. I watched the weather channel incessantly throughout the week before my departure to the monastery for Thanksgiving. Myra advised me to get an early start, so I planned to work just half a day on Wednesday. Then I'd take Harvey over to her house.

I was a little nervous about seeing Charlie again. I didn't quite know how to introduce the new dimension of our relationship with Betty or Amanda, so I hadn't even shared it with them. Frankly, I hadn't had much time to think about Charlie, and I wasn't even sure myself of the emotions I was feeling. I knew that I enjoyed being with Charlie, and I'd like to get to know him better. There's an attraction, but I don't think I could call it love at this point.

I decided not to dwell on what might never be a reality. If our relationship further evolved, I'd keep myself open to other possibilities. In the meantime, I had plenty to do to keep my mind focused.

The skies looked ominous as I packed the car, and there was definitely a feel of snow in the air. A few flurries melted on the windshield as I began my journey to the monastery, but that was about all of the precipitation throughout the trip. I chuckled to myself that the weather people never seem to make a correct forecast. Still, I brought my boots, just in case.

Charlie greeted me at the monastery parking lot, and said that I was the first to arrive. He gave me a little peck on the cheek, and I patted his shoulder. We both felt a little awkward.

Tony hadn't yet returned from the airport with the Sisters from the mid-west province who were coming just for Thanksgiving dinner. Charlie mentioned that the first two Sisters who came earlier in the week seemed to be enjoying their retreat in the poustinias.

"I'm so glad we installed a heat source when we built the cabins," Charlie said. "They can get a little chilly sometimes, but at least they're winterized. I turned on the heat this morning for you and Betty, so your cabins should be nice and warm as you settle in."

Just then, Betty pulled into the parking lot. We timed our arrivals pretty well, I thought.

"Brrr!" she exclaimed, getting out of her car. "We should have put Amanda and Joe in the poustinias. You and I could have stayed in the mansion."

"I thought you liked roughing it."

"I do, but did you hear the weather report? Not to worry though. I came prepared with my boots and extra blankets."

Charlie helped us load our stuff into the golf cart, and then assisted with the unloading when we arrived at our cabins.

"I've got to put the cart into the garage in case it snows," Charlie said, "then I'm going to the diner for supper. Why don't you girls join me?"

It didn't take long for us to head back to the parking lot. Dusk had already arrived. I noticed that the poustinias with the Sisters were in darkness.

"They go over to the big house for prayers and supper," Charlie said. "I've been driving them back to their poustinias around 8 p.m., but tonight they want to stay later so they can chat with the new arrivals. We have plenty of time to go to town."

Jake's Diner wasn't too busy. I surmised that most of the regulars were home making their stuffing and coleslaw. After placing our orders, I told Betty and Charlie about Amanda's rough couple of weeks since the funeral. I explained that she's seemed to find new strength through her volunteer work at the homeless shelter.

"I give that girl credit," Charlie replied. "She's got a lot of spunk. The worst decision I ever made was giving up my boy, but I can't imagine if I'd had to bury him with Stella."

I should have been more sensitive to Charlie's feelings before initiating such a conversation.

Betty looked across the table at Charlie. "She's going through the devastation you felt, Charlie."

"The big difference," I said, "is that Amanda has support. Joe and Kate have become really good friends with Amanda. She has her dad and me, and Father Jim at the shelter has taken her under his wings. Charlie had no one."

Charlie's eyes told me how much he appreciated my comment. Changing the subject, I asked Charlie about the visiting Sisters.

"They seem nice. Sister Gertrude is the talkative one. She asks me all kinds of questions about the monastery and the vineyards. The other one is Sister Bridget. She seems to be really making her stay a retreat."

"Do you think they like the place?"

"What's not to like? They both told me they wish they'd known about the poustinias. Gertrude said she'd like to return in the summer so that she could enjoy the lake."

"You know," I said, "I'll bet there'd be a way to drain some of the lake in the winter so that it could be used for ice skating. That might entice folks to come during the colder months."

"Here she goes again," Betty said.

"It's not too far-fetched," Charlie noted. "Tony told me that when they were novices, the lake would freeze up solid during the winter and the nuns would go skating during their recreation. They'd also go sledding on the hill beyond the parking lot."

"Enough!" Betty laughed. "Don't feed Vicki's imagination. We don't even know the fate of the monastery."

"Let's just hope that tomorrow's dinner goes well. Two of the Sisters in administration from Tony's province will be coming in the morning. I expect they'll have a powwow before the rest of us join them at 3 p.m."

After ordering dessert, the three of us tried to plan our strategy for announcing our donations. We played out several different scenarios until Charlie said, "Let's just wait to see how it all unfolds."

∧∧∧

When I opened my curtains on Thanksgiving morning, I discovered that we'd gotten a coating of snow during the night. It looked light and fluffy, and shimmered on the grassy surfaces. Little paw prints around the yard showed that the squirrels had been scavenging the acorns they were stockpiling for the approaching winter.

By the time I showered, dressed, and had my tea, I noticed that someone had recently swept my front porch and path. I figured Charlie must have been up and about already.

Betty had invited me to her cabin for Thanksgiving breakfast, so I bundled up with jacket and scarf, and traipsed through the woods. The boots weren't necessary, but I passed on my dress shoes in favor of my sneakers.

"My, my," Betty said as she opened her door. "Aren't you a fashion statement?"

I agreed, and pulled a purple knitted cap out of my pocket. I told her she should be grateful that I didn't wear the hat.

"Something smells good in here," I said, glancing at the kitchenette. Betty was cooking a pan of scrambled eggs on the single burner. Bacon had just been taken out of the microwave, and a coffee cake rested on the counter.

"What? You didn't think I could cook?"

"Not at all. I'm just amazed that you thought to bring eggs, bacon, and a coffee cake."

"There's also orange juice in the refrigerator. Pour yourself a glass. If you don't mind, pour one for me and Charlie, too."

I gave her a questioning look.

"Don't be so surprised. I saw Charlie sweeping the porch earlier, and invited him to join us. By the way, don't think I haven't noticed the chemistry between the two of you."

"What chemistry?"

"The winks, the smiles, and the nudges are just the beginning. Remember, I've been trained to read body language."

"I do like Charlie but, as you like to say, I'm just being neighborly."

Betty started to respond, but was interrupted by a knock at the door. "To be continued," she whispered as she opened the door to welcome Charlie.

Betty had everything arranged to seat the three of us. She sat on the end of the bed, I was assigned the chair at the desk, and she asked Charlie to use the stool. We each served ourselves and took turns going back for seconds.

"Thanks for sweeping my porch this morning, Charlie," I said. "How's everything going at the big house?"

"I stopped by to see if I could lend a hand, but the girls have everything under control. All of the visiting Sisters have arrived, and everyone's in a festive mood. Tony told me to tell you that she expects guests to arrive at various times after noon, so the two of you are welcome whenever you're ready."

I told Charlie about Amanda's plan to show Joe and her dad my cabin, for old times' sake. He said he'd be operating the golf cart, and he'd drive them over after getting their bags from the car.

"Is Amanda's dad bringing a significant other?" Betty asked.

"I don't know if he's actually serious with anyone yet. I think he's just started dating this year."

"What's his name?" Charlie asked.

"Steve Angeli. He's a nice guy, probably in his early 40's. Amanda's his only child, and I think he was rather lost after his wife died. He didn't quite know how to deal with a blossoming teen-age daughter who was grieving as much as he was."

"I can relate to that," Charlie said. "I think I was harboring some anger towards him for dropping his daughter here, and leaving her to fend for herself. I never made the connection that I did the same thing with my boy when I couldn't handle my own grief."

"You both did what you felt you had to do to protect your child," Betty replied as she brought each of us a piece of coffee cake.

"I've only met Steve a couple of times, and we've talked on the phone. I got to know him a little better when Amanda was admitted to the hospital last month. I really like him. From what Amanda told me, she inherited more of her mother's artistic personality, but got her love for literature from her dad. He was the quiet one of the family who could get totally engrossed in his books."

"Maybe that's why he thought a place of solitude would be good for Amanda," Charlie pondered, "when, in reality, it made her rebel even more."

Betty and I nodded in agreement.

"Luckily, Vicki was here to guide her," she said.

"I guess I just happened to be in the right place at the right time. Had it not been for that storm we had on my first night in the poustinia, I probably would never have said more than a passing hello to Amanda."

"And, had you not found the brochures Charlie placed in the post office," Betty said, "you would never have even been here. They call that synchronicity."

We all laughed as we began to tidy up the room.

"I know one thing," I said. "This is the finest Thanksgiving morning I've ever had. As Amanda would say, breakfast was awesome, and you guys are awesome."

"I'll second that," Charlie said.

Betty handed him his jacket.

"We girls will do the dishes, Charlie. Go on over and help Tony welcome the guests."

I watched Charlie walk down the path. He had a particularly lively step as he headed toward the monastery. When I closed the door, Betty turned from the sink and said, "OK, spill the beans."

"There's nothing to spill."

"Do you not see that Charlie is falling for you?"

I picked up the towel to start drying the dishes.

"Yes, but I'm not sure that either of us is ready for a relationship."

"What do you need to be ready for?"

"I don't know. It's complicated. I like our friendship, and I enjoy Charlie's companionship. I just don't think I want any more than that."

"All right. Let me ask you this. How would you feel if Charlie had announced that he was bringing a girlfriend to the Thanksgiving dinner?"

"Relieved?" I teased. "Seriously, I haven't ever thought about that.   I'm definitely feeling some emotion—maybe sadness, or even envy."

Betty pulled the towel out of my hands and dried the counter.

"So what's complicated, except for the fact that you haven't dated for so many years that you wouldn't know where to begin?"

"For one, I live two hours away. Heck, he doesn't even have a phone that's not connected to the monastery switchboard."

"Neither of those are insurmountable issues. Get him a phone for Christmas, for heaven sakes. All I'm saying is that I think Charlie and you would be good for each other. Just think about it. Now get out of here while I get myself looking decent enough for the festivities. You've got company coming in just a little while, so you'd better get yourself fixed up, too."

Betty handed me my jacket and scarf. "Thank you for your words of wisdom," I said.

"That's what friends are for. I'll see you shortly. And don't wear that stupid hat."

Chapter 39

Amanda texted me when they arrived at the monastery. I checked my reflection in the small bathroom mirror. My hair and make-up looked nice. I was wearing the pretty top and pantsuit that Amanda had selected for me on her first day of work. Adding the necklace and giraffe pin she gave me, and my dress shoes, completed the outfit. Before long, Charlie beeped the horn on the cart, and I opened the door to Amanda, Joe, and Steve. My appearance was not lost on Amanda as she gave me a big hug, and I welcomed them to my humble abode.

Joe's eyes opened wide.

"Wow! This is cool!" he said.

"I told you so," Amanda replied.

Steve and I chuckled as we watched Amanda point out the things that were identical to the cabin she had stayed in. There wasn't much to make it a grand tour, but Joe seemed to enjoy seeing all that the poustinia had to offer.

"Get your coat, Vicki," Amanda said. "Charlie's going to give us a tour of the place."

We all snuggled into the golf cart, and Charlie weaved through the paths and underbrush to point out the sights. For a man of few words, he was doing a great job as guide. When we got to the lake, Joe was mesmerized.

"You didn't tell me there was a lake."

"I told you there was a lake."

"Well, you didn't tell me it was anything like this! What's under that tarp over there?" he pointed.

"That's our canoe," Charlie replied. "Maybe tomorrow you could help me lug it to the garage for the winter."

"That'd be cool!"

Turning to Amanda, he said, "You definitely didn't tell me about the canoe."

"I didn't know about it, silly goose, but it *is* awesome!"

Laughing, Charlie deftly turned around and took the main road back to the monastery. He pointed out the vineyards, and gave a little lesson on the grape harvesting and wine making. I told them that I had helped pick the grapes during the fall,

"No way!" Joe said. "That's really cool!"

As Charlie pulled up to the front entrance of the mansion, he said to Steve, "Was it like this during your trip here?"

"The whole way."

Sister Tony greeted us at the front entrance, and welcomed us to the monastery.

"It's good to see you again, Amanda and Steve. And this must be Joe?"

Amanda formally introduced Joe to Sister Tony.

Joe said a very proper "I'm happy to meet you, ma'am."

"Likewise," she replied, with a twinkle in her eye.

"Charlie, why don't you come in and get warmed up. You can wait in my office for Jeff and Kim. I'll show our guests to their rooms."

Steve offered to keep him company, and I followed the others to the elevator. I wanted to see the rooms, too. When we got out of earshot, Amanda whispered, "He actually is nice." I cracked up laughing, knowing that she was referring to Charlie.

Tony strategically placed Amanda in the room at the far end of the hall, next to her father's room. Joe's bedroom was near the elevator, across from Jeff and Kim's room. Someone had already brought their bags to the rooms.

I could see what Charlie meant by the wing needing fresh paint. The furnishings were sparse, but the beds looked comfortable. New comforters and fluffy pillows made them appear inviting. Tony pointed out to me that Charlie had purchased a queen size bed for Jeff and Kim's room.

"I told him he didn't need to do that," Tony said. "We were going to move two beds together, but he insisted. He said it was a gift."

"It looks lovely, and it fits perfectly. The half-moon stained glass window above the clear double frame window is very appealing. Look how the light bounces off the colors to make patterns on the wall."

Amanda and Joe had been exploring the bedrooms and bathrooms, and they gave their seal of approval. I could imagine that Amanda was thinking of ways that she could improve the décor, but I was proud of her for being sensitive to Tony's feelings. I reminded them that they were not to intrude on the Sisters' privacy.

Amanda and Joe wanted to use the grand staircase to return to the main floor. Tony and I chuckled when we heard Amanda say to Joe, "I'll be the queen and you can be my bodyguard." He deftly retorted, "I'll be the king and you can be my lady in waiting."

"Waiting for what?"

"Thanksgiving dinner, silly goose!" They bantered all the way down the stairs.

As we made our way to Tony's office, Amanda asked "Do you think the Sisters could use any help in the kitchen?"

"That's a great idea. A few extra hands are always welcome. Let me show you the way."

"It's OK. I remember how to get there. Come on, Joe, wait 'til you see this kitchen. It's amazing!"

Betty was chatting with Charlie and Steve when we returned to Tony's office.

"Those two are a piece of work!" I said.

"They sure are," Steve said. "I could barely get a word in edgewise for the whole trip. You know, when I first saw Joe, I was thinking 'here we go again.' What she sees in all those tattoos is beyond me. But before long, I realized what a nice guy he is. Despite all of their teasing, Joe's very respectful of Amanda. I have to admit that I like him."

Doorbell chimes signaled the arrival of Jeff and Kim. Charlie grabbed his jacket and invited Steve to help him get their bags. After all the greetings, Tony took Jeff and Kim to their room. They, too, wanted to use the grand staircase.

While we waited, I told Betty about Joe's reaction to the tour that Charlie gave. She said that she was so surprised to see Charlie and Steve chatting like they had been long-time buddies.

"For two quiet guys, I'm amazed they found so much to talk about. I'm dying to see the upstairs. Do you think we could go up there?"

"Definitely. It's not B&B quality yet, but it's a great start."

Betty and I joined Jeff and Kim, as Tony showed the upstairs. By the time Charlie and Steve returned, we were ready to join the Sisters in the community room.

A few of the nuns were chatting while watching the televised Thanksgiving Day parade. Four of the older Sisters were playing a card game at the table in the corner, and two more were sitting on the sofa cracking walnuts from the big bowl in the center of the coffee table. Others, most likely, were working in the kitchen.

As Tony introduced us, Amanda arrived with a platter of cheese and crackers, and some napkins. She went from person to person, quite comfortable in her role as hostess.

"You're looking mighty chipper today, Sister Ann," she said to one. "That's a lovely sweater, Sister Elaine. It brings out the color of your eyes," she said to another. There's no doubt that Amanda has a gift of making each person feel special.

Betty and I joined the Sisters on the sofa, while Jeff and Kim mingled with those watching the parade. By the time Charlie and Steve arrived, Tony had brought a few of the nuns from the infirmary in their wheelchairs. Amanda returned with little baked pinwheels and made her rounds.

"Where'd we get these?" Tony asked her.

"Joe's creation. Try one. They're really good."

Chapter 40

Before long, we were called to the dining room for Thanksgiving dinner. Tables had been placed to form a large H, and each place setting included a name card. It was evident that a great deal of planning went into the seating arrangements so that all of the Sisters and guests were mixed and mingled. I wondered whose idea it was to put Charlie directly across from me.

A large platter of sliced turkey breast, adorned with wings, legs, and thighs, was placed in the center of each section of the H. That was surrounded by bowls of stuffing, mashed potatoes, and gravy. Joe seemed to continually bring out more side dishes than I could count. Finally, the kitchen crew emerged, and we gave them a big round of applause. As they found their seats, Tony stood to say the blessing.

"Before we begin," she said, "I want to welcome all of our guests. We are so pleased to have four Sisters from our mid-west province, two of our own administrators, and our friends who have supported us with their visits to the poustinias, and even their work in the fields. Many thanks also to Jeff for his contributions of the canoe, porch accessories, and screen doors for all of the cabins." We all clapped.

"As you know, we're in discussions for a merger of our Sisters and the mid-west branch. We wanted this Thanksgiving to be a very special celebration honoring the past and embracing the future. The Monastery of St. Carmella holds many memories for us. It's the place of our formation, and the burial ground of the Sisters who toiled to preserve our legacy. So, for these reasons, we ask for blessings on our food, and those who worked to provide it, the gift of friendship, and the stability of our beloved community. Please enjoy!"

Platters and bowls were passed around the table family-style. The turkey was moist and carved to perfection. The mashed potatoes were delectably creamy, and the stuffing reminded me of my mother's delicious concoction. I added some corn and green beans to my plate, and tried to fit some homemade cranberry sauce and coleslaw.

There was plenty of chatter between and among all of us as we enjoyed our meal. I watched Joe and Amanda, totally engaged in a conversation with several of the older Sisters. Jeff drew Kim and two of the visiting Sisters into a discussion about his experiences at the poustinias, including the intrusion of a skunk near his cabin porch.

Tony invited each of us to recount a family story about Thanksgiving. I told about the time my mother was defrosting the turkey on the counter overnight. That was bad enough, but worse was that she found the bird on the kitchen floor early Thanksgiving morning, half eaten by our dog.

"Oh, my goodness," Dolores said. "What did she do?"

"She washed it, stuffed it, and put it in the oven. Only after we finished eating did she tell us what happened. It's amazing that no one got sick!"

Sister Gertrude told us about the time her mother didn't realize that she had to remove the bag of gizzards from the cavity of the turkey. Her uncle was the lucky recipient of a heart and a neck bone.

Julie recounted the story of the turkey her father was determined to deep fry in oil. Her mother insisted that he set up the fryer in the backyard, which was a good idea since the whole contraption went up in flames. The turkey was incinerated, and there was nothing left of it once the fire was extinguished.

Around the table, each story was funnier than the previous one. Some actually were poignant reminders of years long past. When we got to Steve, he told us that he really couldn't think of anything. He said he had been adopted as a young child, but both of his adoptive parents had died when he was in grade school. He was in foster homes until he graduated from high school.

Amanda looked at him in surprise. "I didn't know you were adopted, dad. I thought it was your real parents who died."

"They were my real parents, honey. My birth parents abandoned me at some hospital when I was about a year old."

There was a clang of cutlery hitting a plate. Side conversations halted, and Charlie apologized for dropping his fork.

Tony recognized what triggered Charlie's distress, but continued the discussion by saying, "I remember my very first Thanksgiving at the monastery. I was so homesick, and couldn't imagine that our community celebration would be anything like the family gatherings I remembered as a child. After our morning prayers, all of the Sisters who were able went to the kitchen to begin preparing our feast. While the turkey was roasting, we brought Sisters from the infirmary to the community room. The camaraderie was wonderful. I was asked to keep an eye on Sister Dominica. She had diabetes and was blind, but she could still find the candy bowl."

"I remember her," Dolores said. "She had a great sense of humor, and she could tell the funniest stories!"

"She sure could," Tony replied. "I thought I was doing a pretty good job of keeping her out of trouble when, in fact, she was taking me under her wing. She told me of the early days of the monastery. Do you know there was even a bowling alley in the basement?"

"Cool!" Joe said. "Is it still there?"

"Sure is. It's just one lane and you have to stack the pins by hand, but I remember sneaking down to find it. Anyway, she had us all laughing. She and I became friends that day, and that made my first Thanksgiving at the monastery really special."

After each of us around the table shared our memories of Thanksgiving, Amanda said, "That was fun! Let's do it again. Ask another question, Sister Tony."

Tony looked at Charlie, then nodded and said, "Let's have a birthday celebration. The person whose birthday is the closest one following today's date doesn't have to help with the clean-up, and gets the largest piece of pie for dessert. You can start, Amanda."

"Awesome! My birthday is April 4, but I already know that I'm not the winner."

"Yeah, my birthday is April 2," Joe said, "so at least I beat you!"

We continued around the table and Joe was in the lead until we got to Sister Bridget, whose birthday is February 21. Everyone was congratulating her for moving into first place.

"Don't count your chickens before they hatch," Amanda announced. "We haven't gotten to my dad yet."

"When's your birthday, Steve?"

"My birthday is January 10."

Amanda gave her dad a thumb's up. "You may be the winner, dad!" I saw Charlie gaze intently at Steve.

"Not so fast, Amanda," Betty said. "My birthday's December 6."

Betty was declared the victor, and the rest of us cheered.

"Hey, dad. If you were adopted, are you sure that's your real birthday? Maybe your adoptive parents just picked a date they liked."

"Give it up, Amanda," Dolores teased. "Betty won fair and square."

"I'm sure, honey." Steve said. "When I turned 18, I was allowed to read my file. I saw the adoption paperwork. So yes, my birthday is January 10. I'm 41 years old."

Tony had a strange expression on her face. For that matter, so did Charlie.

"Do you know what hospital you were brought to, Steve?" Tony asked.

"Gosh, let me think. I know I saw it in the documents. It wasn't St. Luke's. It was a few hours' drive from here. Is it important?"

"It's not important enough to put you on the spot," Tony said. Let's continue our dinner."

I was watching Charlie from across the table. He didn't take his eyes off Steve. Amanda reached for a serving of mashed potatoes.

"Hey, dad, maybe your real name isn't Steve Angeli."

Joe nudged her arm. She nudged him back.

"This is important, Joe. It affects me, too."

"Don't worry, Amanda. My real name is Steven Aaron Angeli. That was the name on the adoption papers. I don't give a hoot's behind about what my birth parents named me. They obviously didn't want me."

Charlie cleared his throat. "Sometimes things aren't as they seem, Steve. Is it possible that you were brought to Suburban Hospital?"

"Yeah, that's it! Do you know something about my parents?"

There was silence around the table as everyone listened and watched the dynamics between Charlie and Steve. Tony dabbed her eyes with a napkin.

Charlie reached into his back pocket for his wallet. He pulled out a very worn photo of his young son and said, "I think I may be your birth father. My son Aaron was born on January 10. I brought Aaron to Suburban Hospital 40 years ago because I couldn't take care of him after my wife died. I regret that decision every day of my life."

Charlie got up from his chair and walked toward Steve. He handed him the photograph.

"Your birth parents loved you very much. Don't doubt it for a moment."

Steve gazed intently at Charlie, looking for some family resemblance. He studied the picture.

"It doesn't seem possible, but I think this is me."

"I never thought I'd find you." Charlie's voice crackled with emotion.

"This is unreal!" Amanda said. "You think you're my dad's father?"

"I'm sure of it," Charlie replied. "We can have a DNA test if you want, Steve. Aaron favored his mother, and you have the same nose and an identical dimple in your right cheek. I didn't really make the connection when I first met you today, but I know you're my boy."

Tony ushered the men to the kitchen to give them time to talk privately. While she was gone, I told Amanda and the Sisters what I knew about the desperation Charlie faced when his wife died, and how he believed that he had no other option but to ask the hospital to find his son a good home. There wasn't a dry eye around the table.

"So, I'm related to Charlie too?" Amanda gasped.

"Yes. That makes Charlie your grandfather."

"There's more to the story," Tony said as she returned to the table. "My sister, Stella, was Charlie's wife."

"Why didn't you tell us?" Julie asked.

"At first I didn't want to re-live the grieving. Then, I didn't want to compromise Charlie's privacy. Eventually, it just seemed unnecessary."

"So, I'm related to you, too?" Amanda asked.

"I guess you are, my dear," Tony said with a quirky smile.

"Apparently, Sister Tony is your aunt," I said.

"Geez! Who'd believe it?" Amanda exclaimed. We all laughed.

"On that note," Sister Tony suggested, "let's have dessert. I told Charlie and Steve to take a walk. I'm sure they'll be back shortly. It's mighty cold out there."

Several of the Sisters began clearing the table, while Amanda and Joe delivered a piece of pumpkin pie with a dollop of whipped cream to each person. Betty got a double portion.

"Joe made the whipped cream," Amanda announced proudly as she put my dessert plate in front of me. I gave her a little hug.

Charlie and Steve returned, announcing, "It's snowing out there," while brushing a coating from their shoulders. I know it was difficult for Steve, but he looked at the crowd of Sisters and said, "I'd like to rescind my previous statement about my birth parents. I had no idea that my father has been tormented for 40 years because of a freak accident that killed my mother and left him with a decision that no father should have to make."

Steve put his arms around Amanda. "I am honored to introduce my dad, Charlie." We all cheered, and Charlie was beaming.

As we were finishing dessert, Sister Gertrude asked Tony if she might say a few words. Tony nodded her approval.

"Certainly, none of us expected to witness a miracle today. It has made this Thanksgiving Day memorable for all of us. But our experience goes beyond the tangible. Bridget and I had the wonderful opportunity of making a retreat in the poustinias. We prayed with the Sisters this week, walked the grounds, and saw firsthand the vibrant community of the Monastery of St. Carmella. We want to say, first of all to the Sisters, that we're impressed with all that you've done to maintain the integrity of our founder's spirit, while operating a sustainable ministry. Secondly, to the friends who have supported the monastery, it's evident that each one of you has been touched in unique ways, all sharing in the beauty of our Sisters and the work they do. After reviewing the financial records of the monastery this week, and thoroughly discussing the ramifications, we fully embrace retaining the Monastery of St. Carmella as a community asset when our merger is complete."

Everyone cheered. Tony looked relieved. Sister Gertrude waited for all of us to settle down.

"We would also like to commend Sister Tony for her vision and business acumen. The idea of the poustinias is brilliant, as well as the outsourcing of the wine production."

"Did she tell you that we've even been discussing the possibility of turning the west wing into a B&B?" Julie asked.

"Oh, my God," Tony muttered.

"It looks like you've already started one," Gertrude said with a chuckle.

"While some of the Sisters did suggest the idea of a B&B," Tony said, "we haven't yet investigated the cost of renovations that would be necessary to assure privacy for the Sisters. I also don't believe that we'd have the resources to undertake such a project at this time."

"I'm glad you mentioned that, Tony," Jeff said as he stood up. He pulled out a check from his breast pocket. "I'd like to present to you a donation from my company, as well as the companies of several of my colleagues, for $100,000.

"Dear God in heaven!" Tony exclaimed.

Charlie stood up as he reached into his pocket. "Here's a checkbook with over $15,000. This includes money I raised at the Fire House Bingo and selling my birdhouses, donations from Betty and her teens, Vicki's yard sale and, most of all, Amanda and Joe's bake sales." Tony looked at each of us with disbelief.

"Way to go, Aunt Tony," Amanda called out.

I stood up and said, "I have a commitment from my firm for a donation of $25,000. There's more if you need it." Tony looked as if she was going to cry.

Charlie stood up again, and said, "I've sketched out a plan to entirely separate the west wing, if that's what you choose to do. Vicki has a cost and revenue spreadsheet that includes hiring an architect, as well as an estimate of the cost of renovations."

I noticed a number of the Sisters giving high fives.

"I can see why you've been so successful, Tony," Sister Gertrude commented. "With such a team of Sisters and friends on your side, you've created a synergy that will see us forward. You have our support in whatever direction you choose."

"OK, let's get this place cleaned up so Joe and I can take a walk in the snow," Amanda declared.

Tony stood up while trying to compose herself. "Let us thank God for such an amazing day," she said.

We bowed our heads while Tony ended our meal with a Thanksgiving prayer. As soon as the Amens were finished, I rushed over to Charlie and gave him a big hug. He kissed me—on the lips. I kissed him back.

"Dear God in heaven!" Tony exclaimed again as she watched us. "I can't take one more surprise today!"

Epilogue

After Thanksgiving dinner, we all helped bring platters and plates to the kitchen. Still in a festive spirit, there was much chatter and laughing as we shared in the clean-up. Some of the older Sisters retreated to their community room, and Sister Tony invited the other guests to her office. She linked her arm with Steve's, and they led us down the hallway like a scene in The Wizard of Oz.

Tony asked Steve to light the fire in the freshly prepared fireplace, and Jeff asked Charlie to help him get something from his car. They returned with a large-screen smart TV and digital antenna, and began to hook them up to Tony's wi-fi.

"This is a gift for the Sisters," Jeff said, "or for the B&B if you decide to go that route. I figured it's just what we need on a chilly Thanksgiving night."

"That's awesome!" Joe exclaimed.

"Don't get too cozy yet," Amanda retorted. "We're going for a walk in the snow."

"This is a wonderful gift, Jeff and Kim," Tony said. "Thank you so much."

She turned to all of us and said, "I'm overwhelmed by your generosity. Thank you. The Sisters prepared evening refreshments. There's a variety of beverages, glasses, and ice on the corner table, and an assortment of snacks on the bookshelves. The hot water dispenser is on my desk. If you need anything else, I'm sure that Amanda and Joe would know where to find it in the kitchen. Please make yourselves at home."

"Can you stay with us for a while?" I asked Sister Tony.

"Definitely! I want to get to know my nephew. Come join us, Charlie."

The three of them settled themselves by the cozy fire. Amanda rolled her eyes, and handed Joe his jacket. As they bundled up, Amanda said, "This is just too weird. Let's get some air."

Betty and Kim arranged seating around the TV, while Jeff opened a couple of bottles of wine. I brought a glass to each of the guests. Before long, we were all engaged in conversation, barely viewing the football game that Jeff had managed to find among the channels.

Amanda and Joe retuned, rosy-cheeked and shivering. They fixed themselves a cup of hot chocolate, and sat on the floor by the fire, at the feet of Tony, Steve, and Charlie.

I looked around at the scene before me, and reflected on the journey that had brought us together. I had found a simple brochure in a post-office. "Discern where life is leading you," it said. "Come to the Poustinias at the Monastery of St. Carmella, nestled in 383 acres of forest and vineyards. Walk along the stream that feeds the small mountain lake. For the hardy soul, take a dip in the invigorating water that promises to whisk away the cares of the world."

We each had our own story. We each had our own passage of exploration and transformation. I knew in my heart that today was a beginning, not an ending.

I no longer questioned my future. Rather, I savored the confidence that I was on a designed path, my life intermingled with that of my new friends. Who could have imagined that the poustinias would bring us together at the Monastery of St. Carmella? I look forward with joyful anticipation of all that is to come.

ABOUT THE AUTHOR

Kathleen lives in Southeast Pennsylvania with her dog, Pete. She is an educator and a registered dietitian, and has taught students of all ages. Kathleen was a member of the Sisters of I.H.M. for 29 years. Her writing genre of women's fiction is meant to be uplifting, with a focus on women of all ages who are strong, generous, compassionate, and capable. Kathleen's first two novels centered on the Sisters at an imaginary monastery in order to demystify the beauty of a life of dedication and ministry.

Kathleen's characters and settings are drawn from memories of people she has met, and places she has experienced. The poustinia theme was selected because of a week's private retreat at a cabin similar to the one she describes in Poustinia: A Novel. The monastery is reminiscent of her days as an I.H.M. Sister, teaching at St. Aloysius Academy. The Sisters lived in the Drexel Mansion, built by George W. Childs 1891, and bequeathed to George W.C. Drexel. And yes, there was a vintage bowling alley in the basement.

Made in the USA
Middletown, DE
16 September 2017